THE GUNSMITH

#88

THE
TAKERSVILLE SHOOT

The Gunsmith by J.R. Roberts

THE GUNSMITH

#88

THE
TAKERSVILLE SHOOT

J.R. ROBERTS

SPEAKING VOLUMES, LLC
NAPLES, FLORIDA
2015

THE GUNSMITH
#88 THE TAKERSVILLE SHOOT

ISBN 978-1-61232-691-7

For more exciting
Books, eBooks, Audiobooks and more visit us at
www.speakingvolumes.us

Chapter One

Clint Adams was in Takersville, New Mexico, coming from nowhere in particular and going nowhere in particular. Now that his friend Rick Hartman was finally back on his feet, Clint felt that he could take some time to relax. Rick had been injured trying to stop a bank robbery in Labyrinth, Texas. Clint had tracked down the men who were responsible. They would rob no more banks.

He was riding down the main street when he saw the woman crossing the street. She was tall and walked with long, graceful strides. She was dressed like a man — shirt and trousers — but the thrust of her full breasts was obvious, as well as the fact that she had the wide shoulders to carry a heavy load. She wore her hat off her head, held in place by a string, and her hair was long and incredibly black. Her skin was white, which led him to believe that, whatever work she did, it was not outdoors.

One thing he felt sure of, though. This was no saloon girl.

Her long strides were purposeful, and she held herself erect, with her chin held high and proud. She drew the glance of every man on the street, and some of the women, as well — and she knew it. There

1

was no pose of posture on her part, however, even though she knew people were watching. It was as if she was saying, "This is me, take me as I am, because I will not pose for you."

Clint's glance at her was relatively brief, but it made an impression on him, nevertheless, and he vowed to find her again . . . soon.

He drove his rig to the livery, with Duke trailing along behind it.

"Help ya?" the liveryman asked, approaching him.

"Like to put up my rig and team, and my horse," he said.

"Sure thing," the man said, wiping his hands on a rag. He looked as if he doubled as the liveryman and the smithy. He was about six three with arms that were corded with rock-like muscles. He wore a shirt from which he had torn the sleeves, so that his arms were bare to the shoulder.

"For how long?"

"Don't know, for sure."

"More than overnight?"

"Of that much I'm certain."

"Have to ask you for two days in advance."

"No problem."

"Climb on down, then," the man said. He walked around the rig while Clint stepped down, and the Gunsmith found the man admiring his big black gelding, Duke.

"Beautiful animal," the man commented.

"Thank you."

"Is he for sale?"

"No."

The man looked at Clint, then smiled and said,

"Can't say as I blame you." He stuck out a huge hand and said, "The name's Diehl, Tom Diehl."

"Clint Adams," Clint said, accepting the man's hand. The handshake was firm, but the man made no attempt to exhibit what was obviously his superior strength.

"I'll take good care of your stock, Mr. Adams," Diehl said.

Clint asked how much, and then paid Diehl two days in advance.

"Magnificent animal," Diehl said again.

"Speaking of magnificent," Clint said, "Riding into town I saw a—"

Diehl held up his hand to stop him and said, "Say no more. Her name is Carol Sydney. She owns a ranch a couple of miles outside of town."

"How'd you know who I meant?"

"I live here, friend," he said. "When Miss Sydney rides into town, she leaves her horse here. I see her, every trip, and the word that always comes to mind is the one you just used—'magnificent'."

"I see what you mean," Clint said. "Well, you answered my question."

"She the reason you don't know how long you're staying?"

"Could be."

"Can't say I blame you," Diehl said. "Lot of men from town have had a run at her, and lots of strangers, as well. I'll be interested to see if you fare any better."

"So will I, friend," Clint said, with a smile, "so will I."

•   •   •

Clint obtained directions from Diehl to the hotel, then grabbed his rifle and saddlebags out of the rig and headed for it.

On his way into town he'd seen a sign announcing something called *The Takersville Shoot*. He'd meant to ask someone what it was, but the sight of Carol Sydney had caused him to forget to ask at the livery. Now, on his way to the hotel, he saw fliers nailed to walls and posts announcing not only the Takersville Shoot, but something called *The Great Takersville Rodeo and Fair*.

It didn't take a genius to figure out that Takersville was about to be the sight of some big doings. According to the dates on the fliers, the big bash was only a week away.

He wondered idly if he'd still be here then, and guessed that all depended on Carol Sydney.

Only she didn't know it, yet.

"I'm sorry, Miss Sydney," the banker said, "but I just can't loan you any more money."

Carol Sydney gave the banker, Emerson Palmer, a withering glance that said he was more mouse than man.

"My credit is good, Mr. Palmer."

"I'm sorry," he said, "I just can't—"

"You mean Taker *told* you not to loan me any more money," she said accusingly. When she grew angry her brown eyes flashed, and they were flashing up a storm now.

To his credit, Emerson Palmer did not try to lie. He simply spread his hands helplessly and said, "It is his bank, Miss Sydney."

"Bastard!"

Palmer looked shocked, and Carol realized that he wouldn't be able to tell whether she meant him or Charles William Taker.

"Both of you!" she added for his benefit, and then rose and stormed out of his office. She was torn between slamming the door and leaving it open, and ended up leaving it partially open.

Out in the bank proper, people were going about their business calmly, without any idea of the turmoil going on inside Carol Sydney.

Carol decided that she simply couldn't have that.

At the door of the bank she turned, shouted, "Bastard!" and slammed the front door as hard as she could.

She was sorry the glass hadn't cracked, and—for a brief moment—considered smashing it deliberately.

Instead she decided to smash something else.

Like Charles William Taker's head.

Charles Taker sat in his office, wondering if Carol Sydney had yet found out that the bank wouldn't loan her any more money. He'd expected her to come storming into his office by now. He knew full well how beautiful she was when she was angry—hell, she was *always* angry at him—and was looking forward to her appearance with great relish.

Taker was in his mid-forties, a self-made man who had built himself a fortune, and then built himself a town and called it Takersville.

He felt he deserved that, and no one who lived in Takersville felt the need to argue the point. Not when they counted on Charles William Taker for their livelihoods.

One of the exceptions to that rule was the lady he was waiting for now. The lady he wanted more than anything he'd wanted in his life.

Carol Sydney.

Clint had left his gear in his hotel room and then gone in search of the nearest saloon. After he had a cold beer he was going to go looking for Carol Sydney. She affected him at a glance like very few women had, and there was no sense in wasting time looking for her. He didn't know how long it would take, but he'd find her.

He was walking along slowly when suddenly a figure loomed before him and slammed into him. The person bounced off him, looked at him with flashing eyes, and then shouted, "Men!" and kept walking.

It was Carol Sydney.

Chapter Two

"You're late," Charles Taker told Carol Sydney when she burst into his office.

She stood there glaring at him, impressive bosom heaving, her eyes biting into him, cutting him up. She was incredible.

"You've been expecting me," she said accusingly.

"Of course."

"If it's anything I hate," she said, "it's being predictable."

"Carol, believe me, you're anything but that."

Carol Sydney glared at the handsome man seated behind the desk. At one time she had thought there might be something between them, but then she got to know him better. She'd decided a long time ago that there'd never be anything between them except her anger and his arrogance.

"Charlie, you can't do this."

"Sure I can, honey. It's my bank, my town," he said, gesturing expansively, taking in all of their surroundings. "I can do whatever I want."

"You're an incredibly arrogant man, Charlie."

"But you love me."

7

"Once," she said to him, "I might have thought you were amusing, but not anymore."

"Now, Carol—"

"Now I think you're arrogant, egotistical, insufferable—"

"You must feel very strongly about me to have that much emotion—"

"I feel strongly about you, all right," she said. "I feel strongly that this town, this country, would be better off without you."

"Now you know that's not true," he said. "This town *and* this country would die without me. Just look at the people who are flocking in here for the fair, and the shoot. Would they be doing that if it weren't for me? Would the hotel be full? Would the restaurants and the saloons be doing a booming business without me? The stores?"

"We'd all be better out from under your thumb, Charlie."

"It's not under my *thumb* that I want you, Carol," he said, "you know that."

"You want my ranch—"

"I want you."

"And my ranch!"

"All right," he said, "and your ranch."

"Well, you'll never have either, Charlie, believe me," she said. "You'll never have either."

"I believe that *you* believe it," he said, softly, "but it will happen."

"Never!" she spat, and turned and stormed out of the room.

As she left Taker stood up so that he could be seen in the window. The two men across the street came to attention and he nodded. They nodded back, indicating that they had seen him, and understood.

Just a little harassment, he thought, to push her over the edge.

He remained at the window to watch.

Chapter Three

After being run into by Carol Sydney, Clint Adams was torn between going for a beer and following her. He finally decided to follow her, and saw her go into a brick building. As far as he could tell, it was the only brick building in the town. On the second floor there was a large single pane window. Painted on it was the legend: THE CHARLES WILLIAM TAKER COMPANY. He wondered who or what Charles William Taker was, and if she was going in to see him.

She was inside for about fifteen minutes, and then came storming out at the same pace she'd stormed in. It was obviously a bad time to make her acquaintance, and he was about to go for that beer when he saw the two men start across the street. Something in their manner made him stop and watch.

As Carol left the building, she stopped and took a deep breath. It was odd. Where at one time she had thought that there might be a possibility of a relationship with Charlie Taker, she now felt dirty every time she left his presence. She always felt the need for a long, cleansing breath.

She was letting the breath out when she saw the two men crossing the street, and she instinctively knew what was coming. She had never seen them before, but she didn't have to have to know that they worked for Charlie Taker.

She started to walk away, but was too late. One of them mounted the boardwalk and blocked her path, while the other one moved in behind her.

"Let me by," she said testily.

"Hey, missy," the man in front said, "we just want to buy you a drink."

Both men were of a type. Worn trail clothes, two-day growth of beard, foul odor of both body and breath. If Taker were looking to humiliate her, he had chosen his emissaries well.

"No, thank you," she said.

"That ain't polite," the man behind her said, moving closer. If he took one more step she would be pressed up against both of them. The thought made her gag.

"Excuse me, please," she said, putting a hand on the chest of the first man and trying to push him aside. He didn't move.

"Let's have that drink, darlin'," he said, grabbing her by the wrist, "and then maybe you, me, and my friend can go to the hotel and get better acquainted."

"I'd rather chew my hand off at the wrist," she said.

"That ain't pol—" the one behind her started to say again, but he was cut off in mid-sentence. Suddenly he was lifted almost off his feet and tossed into the street, where he went sprawling in the dirt. Another man, much cleaner, neater and better-looking took his place. She studied him, wondering what his intent was, to help her, or take the other man's place.

"I've been looking all over for you," he said to her.

"You have?"

"Yes, the children are ready to go home."

"The children?" she asked, a puzzled look on her face.

"Little Egbert and Melissa," he said. "You remember the children, don't you, dear? *Our* children."

"You got children?" the first man said. He was still holding her by the wrist.

"Who are you, and why are you holding this lady's hand?" Clint demanded. "Is he bothering you, dear?"

"You and her ain't married," the man said. If Carol needed further proof that these men worked for Taker, that was it. If he were a stranger in town, he wouldn't know that.

She saw a smile spread over the other man's face and he said, "I didn't say that we were."

"Wha—" she said, but he nudged her to cut her off.

"Still, I object to the way you're holding her by the wrist. If you don't want to join your friend in the street, I suggest you let her go."

The man looked into the street at his friend, and from the look on his face, Clint knew that the second man had regained his feet and was coming at him. He turned his body halfway and brought his foot up in time to catch the man in the stomach. He went sprawling into the dirt again.

"Let her go," he said to the first man.

"Look, friend—"

"I'm not your friend," Clint said. He looked at

Carol Syndey and asked, "Are you his friend?"

"I'm not his friend," she said, shaking her head, getting into the spirit of the ruse.

"Let her go. "

The man matched stares with Clint for a few moments, and then released her wrist. Immediately she drew her hand back, closed it into a fist and drove it into the man's face.

"What the—" the man said, more stunned than hurt. "Why you—"

"Don't," Clint said sharply. The man had started toward Carol but Clint's one word arrested his movement.

"Pick up your friend and get out of here . . . now!"

For a moment the man stared into Clint's eyes. What he saw there disturbed him enough to force him back into the street, where he helped his cohort to his feet. The two of them hurried off. Every four or five steps they turned and looked back at Clint and Carol.

Carol Sydney turned and looked at Clint.

"Little Egbert and Melissa?" she said.

"I'm sorry," he said, grinning sheepishly. "First names I could think of."

"I appreciate what you did," she said. "That was quite an act."

"Glad to help," Clint said, "but it wasn't totally an act."

"Well," she said, looking at him carefully, "I know there's no Egbert and Melissa, so which part wasn't part of the act?"

He met her eyes boldly and said, "I *have* been looking all over for you."

"You have?" she asked, cocking her head to the left and giving him a quizzical look.

He nodded and said, "Yes, I have."

From his window, looking down diagonally, Taker was able to watch what had happened, and he was incensed. He didn't know who the stranger was, but he had just made a very bad mistake. Nobody interfered with Charles William Taker's business.

The two men across the street looked up into Taker's window, and the man gestured at them angrily to come up to his office.

As he watched further he saw the stranger and Carol Syndey begin walking down the street together.

The stranger's mistake was one he would surely come to regret, as soon as Charles William Taker found out who he was.

Chapter Four

Against her better judgment, Carol Sydney was interested in Clint Adams. He took her mind off her anger, and that in itself was enough of a reason to accept his invitation to coffee.

She led him down the street to a small cafe that she said served the best hot apple pie in the West.

"How's the coffee?" he asked.

"Strong."

"Then let's go."

They went inside and Carol was greeted in a friendly manner by the attractive waitress. In fact, the waitress would have taken all of Clint's attention had not Carol Sydney been present. Carol was the kind of woman—physically—who made other women in the room with her seem to disappear.

"Thanks, Diane," she said to the waitress.

"This a new friend of yours?" Diane asked. She was in her mid-twenties, with long brown hair worn in a ponytail, and a slender figure.

Carol gave Clint a long look and then said, "I'm not sure yet, Diane."

"Well, if you don't want him, let me know," Diane said. "You can toss him my way."

Carol smiled at Clint.

"What would you like?" Diane asked.

"Two apple pies and a pot of coffee, Diane."

"Comin' up." Diane leaned over and tapped Clint on the shoulder. "Don't go away while I'm gone."

"I won't," Clint promised.

As Diane walked away Carol laughed and said, "You seem to have a way with women."

"With women," he said, "or with waitresses?"

"I'm here, aren't I?"

"Why?"

"Why what?"

"Why are you here?"

"I was going to ask you that," Carol Sydney said. She put her hands together, then pointed her index fingers at him. "Why are you in Takersville? For the shoot?"

"I don't know anything about the shoot. What is it?"

"It's a contest," she said. "A marksmanship contest. Draws people from all over the county, and some from out of the county."

"Big doings, huh?"

"Big for the town," she said. "People started filing in yesterday. In three days there won't be a room to be had in a hotel or rooming house."

"What else is happening?"

"A fair and a rodeo. There'll be competition in riding, roping, bulldogging—"

"Sounds like a busy time for everybody."

"It usually is," she said. "People usually forget their problems during the Takersville Shoot."

"But not you?"

"Not this year," she said, "but I didn't come here to talk to a complete stranger about my problems."

"Why did you come here?"

She eyed him for a moment and then said, "You managed to get us back to that question very nicely."

"Will you answer it this time?"

"If you'll answer it after me."

"Deal."

"I came here to forget my anger," she said, "for a little while, and to reward you for helping me."

"With coffee?" he said. "Is that all my help is worth to you?"

"No," she said, "don't forget the apple pie."

"Coffee and apple pie."

"Wait until you taste the pie," she said. "Now you."

"Me what?"

"Why are you here?"

"Just passing through."

"No," she said, "I mean here with me, not here in the town."

"I know what you meant," he said. "I'm stalling, trying to find some way of saying this without sounding like a fool."

"Why don't you just say it straight out?"

"All right," he said. "I saw you when I rode into town, and I wanted to meet you."

She waited a few beats and then said, "That's it?"

"That's all of it," he said. "You impressed me."

"Well . . ." she said, unsure as how to react, "that's very . . . flattering."

At that awkward moment Diane came with the apple pie, and put the largest of the two pieces in front of Clint.

"Thank you, Diane," he said, smiling at her.

"Let me know if you need anything else," Diane said to him.

"I will. Thanks."

When Diane left, Clint looked back at Carol and found her studying him, her chin in her hands.

"What?" he asked.

"It's nothing," she said, shaking her head.

Clint picked up the pot of coffee and poured two cups.

"Come on," he said, " 'fess up."

"All right," she said. "I think you're the kind of man my mother warned me about."

"That's great," he said, rolling his eyes. "What kind of man is that?"

"The kind of man who treats all women like they're something special."

"Women are special."

"All women?"

"Yes," he said, "although admittedly, some more than others."

"Jesus," she said, "you're the kind of man my father warned me about, too."

"And what kind is that?"

"The kind who says what he's thinking, and believes it. I mean, you're not just saying that to try to impress me. You really believe it."

"Of course I do—"

"I know you do," she said, "I could see it in your eyes and on your face when you were talking to Diane. You know she likes you and you gave her just enough attention to make her feel good about it."

"She seems to be a very nice woman."

"But you're not interested in her."

"I could be," he said. "I would be, if you weren't here."

"I could leave."

"I don't mean here in the cafe," he said, "I mean here in the . . . the county!"

"I'm flattered," she said. "Truly, I am."

"Then have dinner with me this evening."

She picked up her fork and cut a piece from her pie.

"I don't know if that's such a good idea."

"Why not?"

"Well, for one thing I don't think I would be very good company."

"I'd like to be the judge of that, if you'd let me," he said.

She studied him, obviously giving the proposition some serious thought. Either that or she was trying to think of the firmest possible way she could say no.

It was possible that all she needed was one final little push.

"I'd hate to call in the debt you owe me," he said. "I was hoping to save that for some later time."

He watched her for a few more seconds, and she nodded to herself, having made her decision.

"All right," she said, "but you'll come out to my ranch for dinner."

"Your ranch?"

"Yes, my ranch," she said. "I'll have you know I'm a woman of some means—or I was until recently."

"Uh, do I get an explanation of that last statement?"

"If you really want it," she said, "you can have it tonight at dinner."

"Fair enough."

"I have to be going," she said, standing up. "I hope I haven't made a mistake."

"You haven't."

"You might just be another masher like those other two, only with better manners."

"I'm not."

She studied him for a few moments, and then said, "No, I'd bet you're not. See you tonight."

"Hey," he said, calling to her as she moved toward the door, "how do I get to your place?"

"Ask anyone," she said. "They'll tell you. You can't miss it!"

Clint watched her until she was through the door, enjoying the way she moved in her jeans, and then became aware of the waitress standing next to the table.

"She's a real nice lady, ain't she?" Diane said.

"Yes, real nice."

"And pretty."

"Very pretty."

"Are you good friends?"

"We just met today."

"Oh," she said, obviously pleased to hear that. "Sort of like . . . us."

"Yes," he said, smiling at her, "sort of like us."

Clint knew he could have this pretty girl in bed in ten seconds if he wanted her, and he'd be a fool not to want her—but then there was Carol Sydney, right there in the front of his mind. Would it be fair to Diane to bed her and make love to her while thinking of Carol? He didn't think so.

He almost asked *her* for directions to Carol's

ranch, but then decided that wouldn't be quite fair, either.

He paid his check, made some conversation with the hopeful Diane, and then left. He wanted to buy himself some new clothes for his dinner engagement this evening.

He wanted to make a real good impression.

Chapter Five

When Clint returned to his hotel, new suit beneath his arm, the hotel clerk, a florid-faced man with a skinny black tie and soiled collar, beckoned him over ominously.

"Mr. Adams, I don't like to, ah, pry into other folks' affairs, but, uh, since you are a guest at the hotel I, uh, felt it my duty to, uh—"

"Spit it out, man," Clint said. The man's halting manner of speaking—whether normal or just evident in this instance—had him leaning forward, waiting for the point to finally be made.

"Well, I'd probably get into trouble, if, ah, if it came out that I, um, *told* you—"

Clint frowned, then took out a dollar and gave it to the man. If the information he was bound to impart wasn't worth the money, he could always wring it back out of him.

"There were two gentlemen—and I use the word loosely—here, asking about you."

"Asking what about me?"

"Your name, when you arrived, how long you intended to stay—"

"And you told them?"

"Well," the man said, looking sheepish, "I did say

that they were gentlemen only in the, uh, *loosest* sense of the word."

And they probably paid him for the information.

Clint described the two men who had accosted Carol Sydney on the street, and the clerk was nodding his head even before he finished.

"Yes sir, that's them, all right. They aren't friends of yours, are they?"

"No, they're not. Tell me about them. Do they belong here in town?"

"They've been here a couple of weeks."

"What do they do?"

"Do?"

"Do they work?"

"Well, I don't know that they have *jobs*, exactly, but I have seen them go in and out of Mr. Taker's office. Then again, Mr. Taker has a lot of people working for him—"

"Taker owns the town?" Clint asked.

"Well, not the *town* exactly," the man said, "but a good portion of the businesses in it, yet—"

"Including the bank?" It had been Clint's experience that the man who owned the bank owned the town.

"Yes, he does own the bank."

Clint was putting two and two together. Carol's remark about being a woman of means until recently, coupled with her coming out of Taker's building— and probably his office—and, then being accosted by two of his men, added up to one thing. If she was having some misfortunes of late, this fella Taker was behind it.

"Thanks for the information," Clint said.

"Sure," the clerk said, pocketing the dollar Clint had given him.

"By the way," Clint said.

"Yes?"

"Who owns this hotel?"

"Why, Mr. Taker does."

Apparently the man didn't see anything suspicious about the fact that he worked for Taker and was selling Clint information *about* Taker and his men.

The man was either an opportunist who would sell out his own mother—or he was acting under instructions.

Charles Taker regarded the two men standing before his desk. He'd imported them only two weeks ago, but already he was prepared to let them go, as soon as they made this final report.

"Well?"

"His name's Adams, Mr. Taker," one of them said. He knew their names were Clyde and Jim, but he couldn't remember which was which.

"Clint Adams," the other said.

"*Clint* Adams?" Taker said.

"That's right."

"Do you idiots know who that is?"

They exchanged glances and then shrugged. Both of them were in their early twenties, and didn't have a brain between them.

"You ever hear of the Gunsmith?"

One of them said, "Yeah, I heard of him," with round eyes. "Is that who that was?"

"The Gunsmith?" the other said. "Ain't he that fella who killed a lot of men? Like Hickok?"

"He didn't kill Hickok, you dope," the first man said.

"I don't mean he *killed* Hickok, I mean he kills *like* Hickok," the second man argued.

"That's enough!" Taker said, before they got too involved in their argument. "You fools are lucky you're still alive after having tangled with him."

"We coulda handled him," the first man said, "only you didn't say nothing about killing. If you want us to we can go and—"

"I don't want you two to do anything," Taker said. He took out some money and gave them each some.

"What's this for?" one of them asked.

"You're fired," Taker said. "Get out."

"Fired?" the second man said, frowning. "What for?"

"Because I hired you," Taker said, "and I can fire you. Now get out!"

Both exchanged puzzled glances, and then they moved to the door and left together. It didn't matter to Taker what they did from now on, whether they left town or not. He was finished with them.

He stood up and stared out the window at the street below.

The Gunsmith, he thought, mentally rubbing his palms together. Fate had played right into his hands this time, hadn't it?

Every year Taker managed to win the Takersville Shoot, which was, of course, named for him. Not *after* him, but *for* him. For one thing it meant he didn't have to pay the prize money out to anyone else. He always managed—some way or another—to come up the winner.

This year it looked bad.

He knew of at least two sharpshooters who were coming to town for the shoot for the first time who could beat anyone he had in his employ. He had tried to find some shooters to import, but had so far come up empty.

Until now.

Now the best damn shot in the West—hell, in the *world*, probably—had come riding into town all on his own, just when Charles William Taker needed him.

All he had to do was hire him.

Chapter Six

Dinner went fine.

Clint was indeed able to obtain directions out to the ranch from almost anyone. He chose to get them from the liveryman, Tom Diehl, who gave him an admiring glance and a wide smile.

"Damn if you didn't get an invite," he said.

"Yep, I did," Clint said. He couldn't help the smile that covered his own face.

"For dinner?"

"For dinner."

"And?" Diehl asked.

"I guess I'll see about the 'and' after dinner, won't I?" Clint said.

"Damn," he heard Tom Diehl say as he rode Duke out of the livery.

Carol's ranch was called the C&S—for obvious reasons—and was about five miles south of Takersville, riding in a straight line. If you rode in a straight line it wasn't the smoothest ride in the world, but you certainly couldn't miss it.

"It's the biggest spread in the county," Diehl had said, "except for Mr. Taker's Bar-T."

"That figures," Clint said to himself.

Clint was impressed with the house as he rode up

to it, even though it was nothing fancy. It was substantial without being showy, and he liked that. It had two floors, with a balcony overlooking the front steps.

As he rode up to the front steps, a man moved over from the corral to greet him.

"Help ya?" he asked. He was a tall, solidly built man in his thirties, who was not wearing a gun.

"I've been invited to dinner," Clint said. "My name's Clint Adams."

"Oh," the man said, and Clint thought that the look that came over his face was a decidedly unhappy one. "Might as well get down, then."

It wasn't the most gracious invitation he'd ever received, but Clint dismounted.

Although the man obviously wasn't very happy to see him, he just as obviously admired good horseflesh.

"Fine-looking animal," he said, moving closer to Duke, who raised his head, stopping the man's progress.

"Thanks."

" 'bout eight, isn't he?"

"About that, yeah."

The man continued to admire the big gelding.

"Puts horses half his age to shame, don't he?"

"That he does."

Clint was wondering what he was going to have to do to get Carol to know he was there when the front door of the house opened and she stepped out. She was wearing a dress that buttoned all the way to her neck, and it was infinitely more becoming to her than any lowcut gown. For one thing it seemed to emphasize the proud thrust of her large breasts—which needed no extra emphasis at all.

When the man standing with him turned and looked at Carol, Clint realized why his appearance had been met with less than great enthusiasm.

The man was in love with Carol Sydney, an emotion which was as plainly etched on his face as it could possibly be.

Clint watched carefully, to see what the relationship between the two was.

"My God," she said, running down the steps. He thought for a moment that she was glad to see him, but her next words dispelled that illusion.

"Is he yours?" she asked eagerly, running right up to Duke.

The big gelding did something very unusual.

He tolerated her touch.

In fact, the big goof leaned *into* it!

"We're sort of partners," Clint said.

"What do you mean?" she asked, rubbing Duke's massive neck with both hands. In fact, it was much more along the lines of an embrace.

"I mean I don't own him and he doesn't own me," Clint said. "If he suddenly took it into his head to go his own way, I wouldn't stop him."

"Oh, but you wouldn't *sell* him, would you?" she asked, her eyes shining.

Clint smiled.

"No more than he'd sell me."

At that moment she seemed to notice the other man for the first time, while he, on the other hand, had been standing by just *waiting* to be noticed.

Clint wondered if he'd had the same look on *his* face the first time he laid eyes on Carol Sydney.

"Oh, Clint, this is my foreman, Bill Wren."

"We've met," Clint said, and the man just nodded to him.

"Would you mind if Bill took care of . . ."

"Duke."

". . . Duke," she finished. "It fits him," she added, patting the big fella's neck. "Bill is excellent with horses, Clint. Would Duke mind?"

"Not as long as he doesn't try to ride him."

"You don't think I could?" Wren asked.

Clint hadn't meant to tweak the man's ego.

"I didn't mean that," Clint said. "He's just never been ridden by anyone but me."

"Never?" Carol said. Now the look in her eyes said that *her* ego had been challenged, as well.

"Never," Clint said. Damn them if they wanted to feel challenged.

"Bill, will you take Clint's horse to the barn?"

"Yes, ma'am."

Bill Wren took the reins from Carol Sydney's hand, and Clint laid a hand on Duke's neck briefly. The big gelding walked off dutifully with Wren.

"God, he's beautiful," she said, turning to face Clint. "If you had told me about him sooner I would have invited you sooner."

"I prefer to be loved for myself," he said.

"Come inside."

He would have liked it if she'd taken his hand and tugged him inside, but instead she just mounted the steps, and he followed.

The entry hall of the house was the same as the outside. It was big, but it wasn't fancy. Her choice of furnishings seem to run to the practical, and there was no sign of the usual female flourishes you'd see in a woman's house.

"Yes," she said, as if reading his mind, "I furnished it myself."

"Has there ever been a Mister Sydney?" he asked.

"I've never been married, and my father had nothing to do with this ranch. I built it up myself, started when I was nineteen. It's taken me fifteen years to get this far—and it may take fifteen days for it to crumble."

Again the ominous implication that things were not going well.

She knew what he was thinking.

"Come on," she said, "I said I'd tell you about it over dinner, and I will."

This time she did take his hand and led him to the dining room.

She had cooked dinner herself.

"I don't have a cook in the house," she said. "I don't have any servants. I don't approve of that."

That was fine with Clint. He didn't approve or disapprove. He had known some houses where the servants were *glad* they were servants. If they weren't, they didn't know what they'd be. He had met an old black man once who said the worse day of his life was when Lee surrendered. He became a free man and didn't know what to do with himself, and was still trying to figure it out.

Clint tasted the chicken she had prepared and said, "The way this tastes, you don't need a cook."

"I could pretend I'm surprised you like it, but the truth of the matter is I *know* I'm an excellent cook.

Maybe when all this is gone I can open a restaurant. I'll go partners with Diane."

He stared at her and she said, "I'm sorry. I've been doing that, haven't I? Dropping remarks without explaining them. I guess I've been waiting for someone I can talk to to come along."

"That's me."

She stared at him and said, "Yes, I think it is."

And she started talking.

Chapter Seven

To make a long story short, when Charles William Taker suddenly showed up on the scene and built his town, Carol was already there, with her ranch started. She and Charles sort of started at the same time, and for a while they were friends.

"We weren't lovers," she hastened to add, "but I won't pretend I didn't think about it. I felt we were both trying to build something, and that a relationship was something we could maybe build together."

She hesitated a moment and then said, "That would have been the worst mistake of my life."

"Why?" he said, just to show that he was listening. Listening was an art. You had to be able to spot the places where you were supposed to say, "Why?" and "Yes," and even "Uh-huh," the spots where you were supposed to nod, and the spots where you were supposed to keep your big mouth shut. Clint had done enough listening in his life that he thought he knew where all the spots were.

"Charles grew a little faster than I did," she said. "I don't know how he did it. I guess he must have had some investors, but he grew and kept on growing, and as he did he changed. He became a different man. Power-hungry and arrogant. He thought that money could buy him anything."

"Even you?"

"Especially me. You know what he did?"

"What?"

"After the town got started and the bank opened and he got rich, he rode out here and asked me to marry him. He said that he thought he had enough money that I'd say yes to his proposal."

"And what did you say?"

"I said that if he had asked me when he was poor, I might have said yes."

"What did he say?"

"He said he'd give me time to think about it," she said. "That was five years ago, and he believes I'm still thinking about it and that I'll eventually say yes."

"And?"

"And he's got a hell of a long wait!"

"Tell me about the ranch."

"The ranch is in trouble," she said. "I won't bore you with the details, but the money going out is more than the money coming in, and my loan comes due in fifteen days."

"And you can't pay it."

"I can't."

"And Taker's going to foreclose."

"Is he ever," she said. "He told me so. He said that if he did that I'd have to marry him."

This was a place for him to keep quiet. She had something else on her mind, and was working on wording it correctly.

"Do you know what I think?"

"What?"

"I think he's behind my recent setbacks. I've had supplies that never showed up, I've had men who quit, I've had stock rustled, and I think he's behind it all. And you know what the funniest part is?"

"What?"

"I think the son of a bitch thinks he's doing it because he loves me."

"Like he had those two brothers bother you yesterday because he loves you?"

"I figured they were his men," she said. "He's just trying to give me something else to think about, confuse me, harass me so I can't think straight."

"And is he doing it?"

She hesitated, then sighed and threw her napkin down on the table.

"He's doing it very well. Would you like some coffee?"

"Sure."

She got up and cleared the table, refusing his offer of help. Following that she brought in a pot of coffee and two cups.

"What do you have to do to turn it around, Carol?"

"That's funny, too," she said.

"Why?"

"We have this Takersville Shoot coming up, you know? I mean, the rodeo events that they're going to have carry cash prizes, and I think some of my men can win them. That'll be their money, though, unless they want to put it into the ranch."

"Buy a piece, you mean?"

"A small piece," she said, giving him an admiring look. "You figured that out, did you?"

"It wasn't hard."

"I haven't approached any of them with the idea, yet. Do you think I should?"

The fact that she was asking his advice meant she was starting to lean on him. He guessed that she'd been needing someone to lean on for a long time, now.

Did he want to be that someone? Did he want to get *that* involved as a result of a chance meeting? He had seen the woman on the street, been attracted to her, and pursued her. He might even succeed in catching her, which meant bedding her—but what came with that?

"I think you should," he said. "Let them know beforehand that they have a chance to buy a piece of the spread if they can win the money. It will be added incentive, and the more of your men you have trying, the better chance you have to win."

"Still," she said, "the top prize money for each rodeo event is only a hundred dollars."

"How many events?"

"Five."

"Would five hundred dollars help?"

"No."

"How much would?"

"Five thousand."

"Five *thousand*?" he said.

She nodded.

Even if he wanted to, he couldn't afford to give her that much. A thousand maybe, drawn from his bank in Labyrinth, Texas, and sent here, but not *five* thousand.

"There's a way I can get it."

"How?"

"Win the shoot."

"The sharp-shooting competition pays that much?" he asked.

"Yes."

"Why?"

"Because that's what brings the people from other counties, other states. That's what brings the *big* names."

Clint had never heard of the Takersville Shoot, but then, he didn't pay much attention to shooting contests. That was *playing* with your gun, and that was something he never did.

He wondered what Rick Hartman, his friend in Labyrinth, would know about it?

"Like what big names?"

"Doc Garfield."

Clint knew Doc Garfield. He was an old buffalo hunter, a dead shot with a rifle, and still carried a Big Fifty.

"I know Doc," Clint said. "He must be nearly sixty by now."

"He's won it once in the past five years."

"Only once? Must be stiff competition."

"It is."

"Who else besides Doc?"

"I don't know all the names, but the money is put up by Charlie Taker, and he rarely has to pay it out."

"Why?"

"Because he usually wins."

Clint frowned.

"Was Doc shooting for him when he won?"

"Yes," she said, "but he never worked for him after that."

"How did Taker manage to beat Doc the other times?"

Carol shrugged.

"Does he cheat?"

"I don't think so," she said. "I think he hires the best gun he can get and hopes for the best."

"Maybe he intimidates some of the other competitors the way he tries to intimidate you?"

"That's possible, too," she said.

"Who does he have shooting for him this year?" Clint asked.

"I don't know."

"And who's shooting for you?"

"I don't know that, either. Several of my men want to try, but they'll be shooting for themselves."

Clint took a moment to drink some coffee.

"Clint," she said.

"Yes?"

She hesitated, as if unsure of herself, and then said, "*You* can shoot . . . can't you?"

Suddenly, uncomfortably, he knew why he'd been invited to the house for dinner.

"You know the answer to that, don't you?" he asked.

Sheepishly she nodded and said, "Yes."

"And that's why you invited me out here?"

She bristled and said, "You're the one who invited me to dinner, remember?"

"With no ulterior motives."

"Oh no?" she said, glaring at him. "Tell me you weren't hoping we'd end up in my bed?"

Now he couldn't very well tell her that, could he?

"That only makes me human," he said. "If I didn't hope for that, what would I be?"

She opened her mouth to answer, then thought better of it. They both took refuge in their coffee until they could figure out their next move.

Chapter Eight

"Look," she said, "I didn't set out to deceive you. When you introduced yourself I recognized your name. That's not so strange, is it?"

"No," he admitted.

"Then you asked me to have coffee. It was while we were talking—when I saw that you were interested in me—that I got the idea of . . . of asking you to shoot for me."

"I see."

"With the Gunsmith on my side," she said, "I can't lose—and I won't lose my ranch."

Clint took his time pouring himself another cup of coffee, and then looked at her over the fresh cup.

"What's in it for me?"

"I—Well, I'll pay you, of course."

"Money?"

"Of course, money," she said, "but you'd have to wait until we collected the prize."

"You mean I don't get paid unless I win?"

"I . . . suppose so."

He shook his head.

"I can't go along with that. If something happens and I don't win, I still have to be compensated for my time."

"Compensated . . . how? I don't have any—"

"Not with money," he said. "You have . . . other resources."

She stared at him for a moment, then as understanding dawned she said, "Oh."

"Is that too high a price for your ranch?"

She stared at him for a few moments, then squared her shoulders and said, "No."

"Then it's agreed?"

She hesitated only a moment, then said, "Agreed."

"Let's spell this out, so there are no misunderstandings later," Clint said.

"All right," she said. She waited for him to go ahead and do so, and when he didn't, she realized that he wanted her to do it.

"If you agree to shoot for me in the contest," she said, "and . . . and you *do* shoot, than I agree to . . . to go to bed with you."

"Win or lose," he said.

"Win or lose," she repeated.

"And if I win I get ten percent."

She hesitated again, then said, "Agreed . . . ten percent."

"All right," he said, "we have a deal."

"And now," she said, "I think you'd better leave."

She had turned cold on him—ice-cold—but he wasn't through.

"There's just one more thing," he said.

He stood up, walked around the table, and pulled her to her feet.

"I want a taste before I leave, just to let me know what I'm waiting for."

"Wha—" she said, but he silenced her with a kiss.

He pressed his lips to hers brutally, and she resisted for a moment, stiff and unyielding in his arms—and then she softened against him. Her lips parted and he thrust his tongue into her mouth. For a brief moment he knew the fire that was buried inside her... and then he released her, just as it was threatening to come to the surface.

She staggered back against her chair, catching herself on the table. Her chest was heaving and her eyes were glazed.

When she found her voice she said, "You're really not that different from Charlie Taker, are you?"

"I'm starting to think that maybe you just bring that side out in a man."

"Get out... get out of here."

"I guess we won't be seeing each other until the day of the shoot," he said.

"And after that," she added, "never!"

He shrugged and said to her, "That's the way it goes sometimes. We could have been friends, but now we're just business partners."

"That's right," she said, "just business partners."

"Good night, partner," he said, and left the house.

He went to the barn to fetch Duke himself. He'd made his bargain with her because she'd stung his pride. She'd only asked him to the house—only accepted his offer of dinner—because of his reputation.

Well, if she wanted the Gunsmith so badly, she'd just have to pay the price.

When Clint returned to town, Tom Diehl was just closing the livery.

"Made it just in time," he said to Clint, accepting

Duke's reins. "You would have had to take care of him yourself."

"I've done it before," Clint said shortly.

Diehl smiled and said, "Didn't go so well, huh?"

Clint studied Diehl and asked, "How long have you lived here, Tom?"

"As long as anybody else. I used to work for Taker until I was able to buy my own place."

"You know Taker pretty well?"

Now Diehl studied Clint for a few moments.

"You thinking about taking him on for Miss Sydney?"

"What if I was?"

"If you were," Diehl said, "you couldn't get anybody better qualified to help you than me."

"Why's that?"

"Because I didn't only used to work *for* Taker," Diehl said, "I used to be his partner."

"Tom," Clint said, "how would you like for me to buy you a drink? Maybe a bunch of drinks?"

"Just let me take care of this special animal," Diehl said, "and you got a deal."

Chapter Nine

When Clint woke the next morning, he felt the pressure of a warm hip against his. It was not an uncomfortable pressure. Quite the contrary, it felt just fine resting there against his, only he couldn't for the life of him remember who it was.

He turned his head and looked over his shoulder. He saw brown hair and a bare shoulder, but he still couldn't see her face. The one thing he did know was that it wasn't Carol Sydney.

That scene came back to him in a rush, and he still felt that he had reacted the only way he could have—with indignation and spite. What man would have acted any other way, right?

He recalled coming back to town and talking to Tom Diehl who told him something important.

Oh yeah, he and Charles William Taker used to be partners. . . .

Diehl took Clint to a small saloon on the other side of town, on a dark side street. This part of town was not the most affluent.

"I drink here," he explained, "because Charlie Taker doesn't own it."

"Hello, Tom," the bartender greeted.

"Two beers, Slim," Diehl said, and steered Clint to a back table. Actually, they could have had any table in the place, as it was empty but for them.

"Who does own this place?" Clint asked.

"A very astute question," Diehl said, as the bartender put two beers on the table before them. "Slim, tell the man who owns this place."

"I do, Tom."

"No," Diehl said, "tell this man who *really* owns this place."

"Oh," Slim said, "you do, Mr. Diehl."

"That's fine, Slim," Diehl said. "Thanks."

Slim—who lived up to his name by being as thin as a reed—went back behind the bar.

"You own this place and the livery?" Clint asked.

"Taker knows I own the livery," Diehl said, "but he doesn't know about this place."

Clint stared at the man and said, "Or any of the others, right?"

Diehl smiled and said, "You are astute."

"You sound like an educated man, Tom."

"Away from the livery, I am," Diehl said. "People expect a man my size, who's running a livery stable, to be on the dumb side. I give them what they want."

"Meanwhile you've been buying up property and business in town on the sly."

"Right."

"Poised to make a move on Taker."

"Right again," Diehl said, "and now my future is in your hands."

"How's that?"

"If you chose to tell Taker all of this, he'd be able to defend himself against me."

"He won't hear about it from me."

"Even if he puts you on his payroll?"

"How would he do that?"

"Look, Clint," Diehl said, leaning forward, "I know who you are, and if I know, Charlie knows."

"So?"

"So, if I know Charlie—and I do—he'll try to hire you to shoot for him in the Great Takersville Shoot." Diehl exaggerated the sound of the shoot's title, making it sound very dramatic.

"He's too late," Clint said.

"Why?"

"I've already been hired."

"By Miss Sydney?"

Clint nodded.

"Excuse me, Clint, but everything I've heard about your rep says you don't shoot for money."

"I don't."

"But in this case you'll make an exception?"

"Nope."

"You're not doing this for money?"

"No."

Diehl frowned and said, "You're not doing it for nothing."

"Not exactly," Clint said. "Carol Sydney and I have an agreement."

"So then you'll be shooting against Taker."

"I guess so," Clint said. "You wouldn't happen to know who's shooting for him, would you?"

"No one, yet. With you in town he'll be after you with money coming out of every pocket."

"He'd better tuck his money away," Clint said. "It isn't going to do him any good here."

"You don't know how glad I am to hear that," Diehl said. "Slim," he called, "bring us a bottle of whiskey over here, and two more beers!"

"Are we celebrating something?"

"We sure are," Tom Diehl said. "The imminent fall of Charles William Taker."

Clint remembered them going through one bottle of whiskey and a few more beers, and still no one else entered the saloon. Finally, as he was getting ready to leave, the batwing doors opened and someone stepped in.

A woman. She waved to the bartender and walked right over to their table.

"Here you go, Tom," she said.

It was Diane, from the cafe.

"Thanks, Diane," Tom said, accepting a sack from her. Diehl saw Clint watching them and said, "Today's receipts," with a smile.

"You own the cafe?"

"Yep," Diehl said. "My most successful endeavor, thanks to this little lady, here."

Diane smiled shyly, not taking her eyes off of Clint.

"Listen," Diehl said to Clint, "you were just getting ready to leave; why don't you walk Diane home? This end of town isn't the most safe, you know?"

"Sure," Clint said, standing up, "come on, Diane."

"We'll talk again tomorrow, Clint. Good-night."

"Good-night, Tom."

Diane leaned over and kissed Tom Diehl on the cheek.

"Good-night, Daddy."

That was as much of a surprise as anything else.

Apparently, the people in town didn't know that Tom Diehl was Diane's father. Diane was using her mother's maiden name—Grant.

So now he knew who the girl in bed with him was. He thought back to their walk from the saloon. . . .

"You don't live with Tom?" he'd asked.

That was when she explained that no one knew that she was his daughter.

"My mother left Papa when I was little, and when she died I came out here to join him. Right away he told me he wanted to run the cafe, but that he didn't want anyone to know we were related."

"How did you take that?"

"After he explained it to me, I understood. You see, my mother left him because he became partners with a young man named Taker."

"Taker must have been young if you were little."

"That was . . . about fifteen years ago, when Taker was in his early twenties. Even then my mother could see what kind of man he was going to become. My father wanted success, though, so he joined Taker, and my mother took me and headed East. I think my father thought that when he had money she'd come back. She never did because he never did, and then she finally died."

"I'm sorry."

"She was unhappy, and blamed my father for it, but I never did. I always wanted to know him. Now I do, *and* I'm helping him."

Clint looked up and suddenly realized that they were standing in front of his hotel.

"This isn't where you live," he said.

"No," she said, giving him a level look, "it's where you live. My place is too small."

"For what?" he asked.

She took hold of his arm and said, "For whatever..."

"Whatever," turned out to be a lot, and her place would indeed have been too small for the things they did during the night....

Clint moved his hip away from hers and turned over so that he could press against her from behind. He slid his penis along the cleft of her buttocks and felt himself begin to swell. She moaned, wiggled against him, then reached behind her to take hold of him.

"Do you think this is what your father had in mind when he suggested I walk you home?" he asked, pressing his lips to the back of her neck. Her hair held the odors of all of the food she'd prepared the day before, but he didn't find it unpleasant. There was nothing he found unpleasant about this energetic young woman.

"I'm sure it was," she said. "It was what *I* had in mind, I know that."

She turned over and snuggled up against him.

"I don't know what happened with you and Carol, and I don't care. Okay?"

"Nothing happened," he said.

"I said I didn't care," she repeated.

"I know, but—"

She silenced him with a kiss that lengthened and grew in intensity until she was on her back and he was atop her. Without breaking the kiss he slid into her and slid his hands beneath her to cup her buttocks. Holding her like that, he controlled the tempo of their lovemaking, pulling tightly against her and then letting her go, then pulling her back again. She wrapped her legs around him and just held on, content to let him dictate the pace.

Soon she began to moan into his ear and then when she came she bit his shoulder, marking him, crying out against him. . . .

"There," she said to him later, rubbing the mark. "Now she'll know someone else was here."

"I thought you didn't care."

She smiled and said, "I lied."

Chapter Ten

Diane wanted to take Clint to the cafe and cook him breakfast, but he told her he'd rather buy her breakfast at the hotel.

"The food may not be as good," he reasoned, "but at least we won't be interrupted."

"All right," she said, "but you'll have to explain to Daddy why I opened late this morning."

"I think your father is already aware of that, Diane," he said.

Over breakfast she told him about her life back East, living with her mother in Philadelphia.

"She was always trying to turn me against my father—or the memory of my father—but I didn't let her."

"Good for you."

"What few memories of my father I did have were good, and I wanted to hold onto them until I could be with him again."

"When did you come out here?"

"Last year."

"Were you here for last year's shoot?"

"Oh, yes. You watch the town start to fill up

today, with the shoot only five days away. You're lucky you got to town early."

"Well, I didn't have any plans to stay when I rode in," he said, "but now those plans have changed."

"You're helping Carol, aren't you?"

"Diane—"

"Clint," she said, putting her hand over his, "don't think you have to spare me anything. I know you're not going to fall in love with me and stay here. I also know you're not going to fall in love with Carol—at least not enough to stay. What you do with Carol—or for her—is between you and her. I just want you to know that I like her, and I'd like to be like her. If you're helping her to keep her ranch, I'm glad."

"Well, it started out that way," Clint said, "but now it looks like I might also be helping your father."

"Well, you certainly won't hear me complain about that."

They finished their breakfast and left the dining room together. In the lobby, the clerk—the same clerk from the other night—beckoned to Clint to come over to the desk.

"I have a message for you, Mr. Adams."

"Well, give it to me," Clint said, putting out his hand.

"It's not in writing," the man said. "It's from Mr. Taker."

"What's he want?"

"He'd like you to come over to his office some-time today, for a talk."

"Fine," Clint said, "tell him that you gave me the message."

As Clint turned away the man said, "You are going to see him, aren't you?"

Clint looked at the man and said, "It's possible, yes. Why?"

"I was just, uh, wondering—you wouldn't, uh, tell him about the other day—"

"Look, friend, whatever you've got going is your business," Clint said.

"Well, uh, yes, I appreciate that..." the man said, and Clint walked away from him.

"Anything wrong?" Diane asked him.

"Just a message."

"From Carol?"

Clint laughed.

"I don't think I'll be getting any messages from Carol in the near future."

"Aren't you helping her?"

"Sure," Clint said, "but that doesn't necessarily make us friends."

Diane frowned, not understanding, and Clint certainly didn't want to tell her about the arrangement he had with Carol Sydney, so he changed the subject.

"The message was from Taker."

"Taker?" she said. "What does he want?"

"He wants to see me."

"Clint," she said, grabbing his arm, "he's going to try to buy you."

"I know."

She bit her bottom lip—the one *he'd* been biting a little while ago—and said haltingly, "He can't... can he?"

"No, Diane," he said, softly, "he can't."

"I'm sorry for asking but—"

"Forget it," Clint said. He'd used up his quota of

indignation on Carol Sydney last night. As far as Diane knew, Charles William Taker could usually buy whatever he wanted.

He took her hand and said, "You're entitled to ask."

"Are you going to see him?"

"Hell yes," Clint said, "I wouldn't miss it. Just because I'm not going to *accept* his offer doesn't mean I don't want to *hear* it."

Chapter Eleven

Before going over to Taker's office, Clint stopped at the telegraph office and sent off a message to Rick Hartman in Labyrinth. Rick had so many contacts throughout the country that Clint would probably be able to ask him who he had spent the night with last night, and Rick would come up with Diane's name.

He sent off a terse message, asking for any information on one Charles William Taker. Of course, there was the chance that Taker would hear about the message, but Clint wasn't really concerned about that. Taker had probably checked up on him, as well.

Clint left the telegraph office and walked over to the building where Taker had his office. He went up to the second floor and knocked on the door that had Taker's name on it.

"Come in."

Clint entered and found himself in an expensively furnished office. The man behind the desk was in his thirties, handsome and handsomely dressed in a three-piece suit.

"Mr. Taker?"

"That's right."

"I'm Clint Adams. I understand you have a desire to talk to me about something?"

"Clint Adams," Taker said, leaning back in his chair. "You don't know what a pleasure this is."

"Why is that?" Clint asked.

"Well, it isn't every day you get to meet a true legend of the West."

"Are we talking about me, or you?"

Taker laughed.

"I see you're modest. I hadn't heard that about you."

"What have you heard about me?"

"Who hasn't heard about the Gunsmith?" Taker said. "The truest shot in all the—"

"I have to tell you, Mr. Taker, you're not making any points with me going on like this."

Taker fell silent and stared at Clint.

"All right," he said, finally. "I guess you're a man who likes to come straight to the point."

"That would be refreshing."

"Very well," Taker said. He opened the top drawer of his desk and took out a long white envelope. He then tossed it so that it landed on Clint's side of the large-topped oak desk.

"What is that?"

"That's five hundred dollars."

"Is that supposed to be for me?"

"Yes."

"And what am I to do for this money?"

"You know about the Takersville Shoot?"

"How could I not?" Clint said. "I've been in town for twenty-four hours."

"I've chosen you to represent me in the contest."

"For five hundred dollars."

"A down payment," Taker said. "You'll get the other half after you win."

"And if I don't win?"

"Please, Mr. Adams," Taker said. "You can carry modesty too far."

"Suppose a bird shits in my eye just as I fire, and I miss and lose?" Clint asked. "Humor me?"

"Very well," Taker said. "In the unlikely event that you do lose, I will pay you anyway."

"I see."

"But I'm quite certain that you will win."

"I don't usually compete in these types of competitions."

"These types of competition don't usually pay this kind of money."

"Really?" Clint said, ignoring the envelope. "I heard that the first prize for this contest was *five* thousand dollars."

"It is," Taker said. "That's common knowledge. I'm not trying to deceive you, but you'd have to expect me to take most of the money, since you'll be working for me."

Clint made a show of frowning. "But I'll be doing all the work."

"That's true," Taker said, nodding, "that's true. All right, I'll make an arrangement with you that I've never made with anyone else." Taker paused, and Clint waited. Finally Taker said, "Half."

"Half?"

Taker nodded.

"We'll split right down the middle."

"Fifty-fifty."

Taker nodded again.

"Well, that's pretty generous," Clint said.

"I think so," Taker said, "but it will be worth it to me to be represented by the Gun—"

"But answer me this."

"What?"

"Why don't I just represent myself and win all five thousand, and not have to split it with anyone?"

Taker frowned.

"You could do that, of course," Taker said, "but after this conversation, I wouldn't advise it."

"Why not?"

"Well," Taker said, "let's just say I wouldn't want my show of good faith—" and he nodded at the envelope on the desk—"to be thrown back into my face."

For the first time, Clint looked at the envelope, as if he was considering the offer.

"No," he said, "I really can't see my way clear to take you up on your offer, Mr. Taker."

"Why not?" Taker asked. "Going after the money yourself wouldn't be worth the hassle, Adams. I can assure you of that."

"I will be going after all the money, Taker," Clint said, "but not for myself."

"For whom, then?"

"I've already agreed to represent someone."

"Wh—" Taker began, but he stopped short when he realized the answer. "Carol Sydney?"

"Correct."

For a moment Clint thought Taker was going to lose his temper entirely. His face turned red and his hands dug into the sides of his chair. He watched the man bring himself back under control with terrific effort.

"That wouldn't be advisable either, Adams," he finally said, his voice deceptively soft.

"It can't be helped," Clint said. "I've already accepted her offer."

"Go after the money yourself," Taker said.

"You just told me that wouldn't be—"

"I'd rather you went after it for yourself," Taker said. "I'll allow that."

"You'll *allow* it?" Clint said. "You arrogant bastard, what makes you think you have anything to say about it?"

Taker's eyes turned into slits.

"I own this town, Adams," Taker said. "I own the county."

"That must be fun for you," Clint said, and moved to the door, "but I don't live in *your* town, or *your* county. I gave my word to Carol Sydney, and I'll stand by it."

"I'll double the money!" Taker said.

"No deal."

"That's ten thousand dollars, Adams," Taker said, standing up. "How can you turn that down?"

"I wouldn't work for a man who'd send two low-lifes to harass a woman."

Clint opened the door to leave.

"What did she offer you, Adams?" Taker demanded. "What did she already give you, huh?"

"That's none of your business."

"You don't have any idea who you're dealing with," Taker said. "Stay away from Carol Sydney."

"Good day, Taker."

"I'll break you, Adams!" Taker shouted as Clint left. "You're just a two-bit gunman, and I'll break you."

Clint turned and asked, "Does this mean you're not glad to meet me anymore?"

After Clint Adams left his office, Charles William Taker closed his eyes and leaned his head against the back of his leather chair. He was trying to *maintain* the control he'd exerted while Adams was still in his office.

Clint Adams was a danger to him now. If he won the contest, Carol Sydney would have the money to pay off her loan, and Taker wouldn't be able to take over her ranch—and her!

Worst of all, Adams would show people that he *could* be opposed.

He couldn't allow that, no matter what he had to do.

And whatever he was going to do, he had five days to do it.

Chapter Twelve

Clint went from Taker's office to Tom Diehl's livery stable.

Diehl looked up from a horse he was shoeing as Clint entered.

"'Morning," he greeted.

"Good morning," Clint said. He touched his head and said, "You're a man who knows how to drink."

"I've had a lot of practice," Diehl said, straightening up. "After Diane's mother left me, I fell into a bottle. Working with Charlie Taker, I fell even deeper. Finally, when Taker swindled me, I hit bottom. I'm still trying to climb out."

"Is that what last night was about?"

Diehl smiled.

"Part of my therapy is to see if I can drink as much as I want, and stop. Besides, last night I was celebrating finding a worthy partner."

Clint did not respond to the last statement.

"We are going to be partners in this, aren't we?"

"That depends on what *this* is," Clint said.

"The destruction of Charlie Taker, of course."

Clint hesitated, then shook his head and said, "Then no, we aren't going to be partners."

Diehl took off his apron and dropped it to the

floor. He slapped the horse on the rump, sending it into a stall.

"I don't understand," he said.

"I didn't come here to get involved in other people's personal problems, Tom."

"What about Carol Sydney?"

"I backed into that," he said, "but I'm not opposing Taker. I'm helping Carol keep her ranch."

Diehl made a violent swipe at the air with his big right hand.

"Same difference. If you're helping Carol Sydney, you're opposing Taker."

"I don't look at it that way."

"Then you're a fool," Diehl said, "because that's the way *he's* going to look at it. Diane says you went to see him today?"

"I did."

"He make you an offer?"

"He did, a thousand dollars to shoot for him."

"And you turned him down?"

"Sure. I told him I could shoot for myself and keep the whole five thousand."

"And then you told him you were shooting for Carol Sydney."

"Yes."

"You'd have been better off letting him think you were shooting for yourself. He's going to come after you, Clint. You can count on it."

"I'm sorry I can't help you, Tom."

"Don't be sorry," Diehl said. "The time will come when you'll resolve yourself to the idea that you're against Taker. When that time arrives, come and see me. We'll be partners then."

"No hard feelings?"

"Hell, no," Diehl said. "I wouldn't want a part of somebody else's fight, either—but pretty soon this'll become your fight. Come and see me, then."

"I hope I can come and see you, anyway," Clint said. He liked the big liveryman.

"Sure, we can have a drink. No problem."

"I'm glad you understand."

"I understand better than you do, lad," Diehl said.

"I'll be seeing you," Clint said, and turned to leave.

"How'd you get on with my daughter last night?"

Clint turned and looked at the man, wondering what he *knew* and what he was assuming.

"She's a real nice girl."

"That she is. She thinks a lot of Carol Sydney, too."

"So she told me."

"Uh, I suppose we can trust you with our little secret?"

"Of course you can," Clint said. "I'd have no reason to tell anyone."

Diehl nodded and said, "Thanks for that." He looked around him and said, "I've got work to do. Be seeing you."

"Sure," Clint said, and left.

Diehl watched as Clint left, then picked up his apron and put it back on.

He knew Clint would be back. Charlie Taker wouldn't leave him any other choice.

Clint was glad the man hadn't become angry at his refusal to help him. If his actions helped the man, that was one thing, but he didn't actively want to take part in the man's vendetta against his ex-partner.

Carol Sydney was another story.

Clint wondered if he should go and see her and smooth things out between them. He was sure they had both said some things they didn't mean last night. He considered it, then decided against it. Let it stand the way it was. They had made a bargain, and they would both stand by it.

Knowing what was in store—or *wondering* what was in store—might give him some added incentive to win the damned contest.

The Takersville Shoot would be his first such contest—and his last.

Chapter Thirteen

Clint went to the cafe for lunch, but Diane was too busy to sit and talk to him until most of the lunch crowd had left. Already that morning he had seen the difference in the town. There were more people on the street and in the stores, and there were more wagons moving down the main street.

The crowds were starting to flow in, just as Diane had said they would.

"This place certainly does better than the saloon," he commented as she sat.

She brushed a stray hair out of place and poured herself a cup of coffee from his pot.

"You do all the cooking yourself?" he asked.

"Most of it," she said. "If it gets real busy I can get help, but we prefer to keep the staff down to one. As for the saloon, it has its regulars."

She had brought herself a piece of the apple pie when she brought him his and now they both started to eat.

"Did you see Taker?"

He said he had and told her about their conversation.

"Have you seen your father today?" he asked afterward.

"No, why?"

"I went to see him after Taker," he said, and then related the conversation *they'd* had.

She concentrated on her apple pie for a few moments then looked at him.

"He's right about one thing," she said.

"What's that?"

"Taker won't allow you not to take sides," she said. "He'll force you into it."

"He'll try."

"That's just it," Diane said. "He *won't* be trying. If anything, he'll be trying to get rid of you, but he'll only succeed in forcing you to go against him."

"Maybe he'll force me to leave?" Clint said. "Did you ever consider that?"

She gave him one of her warm, understanding smiles and said, "No, I never have."

"You think you know me that well after one night?"

"I know you well enough to know why you're still here at all, and it sure isn't because of me."

"Diane—"

"There's no reason for you to respond to that," Diane said. "I understand. Carol Sydney is everything I'd like to be—beautiful, sophisticated, confident—"

"All of those things will come," he said, "but you're already beautiful."

"I'm pretty," she said, "I know that, but not the way Carol is. I see the way men look at me, and I've seen the way they look at her. I don't fool myself, Clint, and I wouldn't want you to try to."

"I wouldn't do that," he said. "If I did, I might not get any more of this pie."

"Want another piece now?"

"I could be talked into it."

She smiled and said, "Coming up."

She got up and went to the kitchen to get the pie. She was right, of course. Carol Sydney was the reason he was still here, and it wouldn't be right to try and convince Diane otherwise.

He liked this girl's directness and honesty. He should tell her that in that respect, she was ahead of Carol.

Look at that, he thought. Still holding it against Carol that she knew who you were all along.

How long would it take to forget that?

Charles William Taker read the telegraph message that Clint Adams was sending to Texas. He didn't know who this Rick Hartman was, but apparently the man must have had some contacts.

"Shall I send it, Mr. Taker?" the clerk from the telegraph office asked.

"Sure, Willie," Taker said, handing it back, "send it. No harm in sending it."

"Yes sir."

"And send these," Taker said, handing the man a bunch of slips.

"Yes sir," the man said, accepting them without question.

After the man had gone Taker sat back and thought about Clint Adams. Let the Gunsmith look into his past. There was nothing there that Charles William Taker was afraid of, or ashamed of.

Maybe this way Adams would finally realize who he was dealing with.

• • •

After lunch Clint went to the telegraph office.

"No reply yet?" he said to the clerk.

"No, sir," the man said nervously.

Clint knew better. The clerk either hadn't sent it yet or had checked with Taker before sending it, which was holding up the reply.

"Well, when it comes in, send it to my hotel, will you?" Clint asked.

"Sure, Mr. Adams. As soon as it comes in."

Clint stood there and stared at the man, causing him to fidget some from foot to foot.

"Must be some trouble with the lines," the man said, forcing a smile.

"Must be," Clint said, and left.

Chapter Fourteen

Later in the evening, while Clint was trying to decide where to have dinner, the response to his telegraph message was delivered to his hotel. When he came down and checked with the clerk—a different man, this time, who seemed quite willing to do his job and nothing more—he accepted it and sat down in the lobby to read it.

C.A.

TAKER SELF-MADE MAN. SMART, RUTHLESS, AND MEAN. SUGGEST DEALINGS WITH HIM BE ENTERED INTO WITH CAUTION. MORE TO COME.

R.H.

He folded the message and tucked it into his pocket. Not much to go on, really, but the advice was there. Deal with caution. Clint liked to think that he had already decided that.

He decided not to have dinner at the cafe. He didn't want to lead Diane on in any way, and constantly eating at her place might suggest to her an intimacy he didn't mean. As levelheaded as she appeared to be, she was still a woman.

75

He decided to have dinner in the hotel dining room.

Wade Barker had been sheriff of Takersville for about three years. He was thirty-one, young for a sheriff, younger still when he had been appointed to the job by the town council—at the direction of Charles William Taker.

Taker wanted a man he could control, but he also wanted a man who had some intelligence and initiative—*some*, but not a whole lot.

Wade Barker fit the bill perfectly.

Barker was tall and good-looking and, in some ways, reminded Taker of himself at a similar age. Of course, at thirty-one Taker was already on his way to becoming a rich man. Wade Barker at forty-one would probably be at the same stage in his life that he was at thirty-one.

Barker entered Taker's office with hat in his hand. Taker thought it was fitting.

"You wanted to see me, Mr. Taker?"

"Wade," Taker said, "how many times do I have to tell you to call me Charlie?"

"Oh, sure . . . Charlie." Barker was clearly uncomfortable with the name and would revert to "Mister Taker" at his earliest convenience.

"I did want to see you, Wade," Taker said. "It's about a man here in town, a stranger."

"What about him, Mr. Taker? Who is he?"

"His name's Clint Adams. Does that name mean anything to you?"

"Adams?" Barker repeated. He frowned, then brightened. "Sure, isn't he the one they call the Gunsmith?"

"Does that impress you?"

With bravado Barker said, "No, why should it?"

"It impresses a lot of people," Taker said. "Hell, it impresses me."

"He's here in town?"

"He is, and I'm afraid his presence might cause trouble."

"You want me to send him on his way?" Barker asked. "It wouldn't be no trouble."

"No, Wade, I don't want you to cross swords with this man. All I want you to do is let him know that you're aware he's here. If he knows you're watching him, then that alone might head off trouble. Do you understand?"

"Sure, Mr. Taker, I understand."

"All right, go on then, and be careful. He didn't get that reputation from scaring easy."

"Yes, sir."

"Oh," Taker said, waiting until Barker was almost out of the room. "One other thing."

"What's that?"

"He's only been here one night, but I understand he's already seeing that girl from the cafe. You know, that pretty one—"

"Diane?" Wade Barker said, closing the door again. "He's seeing Diane Grant?"

Taker could see the look of betrayal on the man's face. It was a well-known fact that Sheriff Barker was sweet on Diane Grant.

"That's what I hear, Wade," Taker said, "that she was seen going into the hotel with him last night, and then coming out this morning."

With a shaking hand—shaking with rage, not fear—Wade Barker put his hat on and once again opened the door. Taker could see that the knuckles on the hand that was holding the knob were white.

"Don't you worry none about this man, Mr. Taker," the young lawman said, "I'll take care of it."

"He's staying at the hotel down the street—" Taker called after him, but the man was gone.

There was nothing like jealousy to fuel a young man's anger. If Barker killed Adams, that would solve the problem, but if Adams killed Barker— well, that would take him out of the contest, too, wouldn't it?

With something akin to amusement, Charlie Taker once again picked up and read his copy of the reply to Clint Adams's telegraph message.

He still didn't know who Rick Hartman—who had signed "R.H."—was, but the man gave damned good advice.

Chapter Fifteen

Unbeknownst to Taker, instead of going straight to the hotel, Sheriff Wade Barker went to the cafe to confront Diane Grant.

He approached her while she was taking an order and said, "I have to talk to you."

"You'll have to wait—" she started to say, but he grabbed her by the arm and pulled her away from the table, saying, "Excuse me," to the two elderly women there.

The two women smiled at each other.

Ah, young love . . .

Barker dragged Diane into her kitchen and only then released her arm.

"That hurt," Diane said, rubbing herself. She knew she'd have bruises from his grip.

"What's this about you and Clint Adams?"

She raised her chin defiantly and said, "What about him?"

"I heard—" he started, then lowered his voice and said, "I heard you were in his hotel with him last night."

"What if I was?" she asked. "That's my business."

"Diane, you know how I feel about you!"

"And you know I don't feel the same way about you, Wade."

"But you could, if you gave it half a chance."

"Wade," she said, "we've had this conversation before. I don't want to get serious with you."

"But you do with Clint Adams, a man you met only yesterday?"

"I don't want to get serious with him, either."

"You don't call staying in his room all night getting serious?"

"Only someone with ideas as old-fashioned as yours would think that."

They'd argued before about his prudish mind and antiquated ideas before.

"Diane—"

"I have work to do, Wade."

He clenched his jaw, then said, "Well, so do I. I have to go and see your Mr. Clint Adams."

"Don't do anything stupid, Wade," she said. "He's not here looking for trouble."

"Any time a man with a reputation like his comes to town he's looking for trouble."

"He's not like his reputation at all."

"No, not that he showed you. He only showed you his sweet-talking side, the side that got you into his bed like a bitch in heat."

She slapped him then, a resounding slap that hurt both her hand and his cheek, which quickly reddened.

"You'll be sorry you did that," he said. He whirled and left by the back door.

Diane's first urge was to leave and run to the hotel to warn Clint, but she had a business to run. Clint

Adams could certainly take care of himself.

That part of his rep must surely be true.

Clint saw the lawman as soon as he entered the hotel dining room. It reminded him that he'd meant to check in with the local law today, but he just hadn't gotten around to it yet.

It looked like that failure was about to be resolved, as the sheriff approached his table.

"Are you Clint Adams?" the man demanded.

The first thing that Clint noticed was that he seemed young to be a sheriff. Maybe he was older than he appeared to be.

The second thing was that the man seemed inordinately angry—and he had a red welt on his right cheek—no, not a welt, more like . . . the outline of a hand.

"I am," Clint said. "Have a seat and a cup of coffee, sheriff. I've been meaning—"

"I just want you to know," the lawman said, cutting him off and pointing at him, "that we don't tolerate troublemakers in this town."

"Well, that's fine, because I'm not—"

"And we don't like fancy talkers coming here and taking our women into bed."

"What?" Clint asked, totally confused. "Sheriff, do you have the right Clint Adams?"

"You're the Gunsmith, aren't you?" the man asked. "Big man with a big rep."

"Now look—"

"My name's Sheriff Wade Barker, and I'll know every move you make while you're in my town, Adams. Don't forget that!"

"Sheriff—"

The man turned and started away from the table, then abruptly whirled on him, shaking with what appeared to be pent-up rage.

"And stay away from Diane Grant!" he said, and stormed out of the room.

Clint looked around the room and saw the other diners staring at him.

All he could do was shrug helplessly and go back to his meal.

Chapter Sixteen

In his office Charles William Taker now had six telegraph messages spread out on top of his desk. One was the reply Clint Adams had received from Texas. The other five were replies to five messages Taker had sent out. His initial hope had been that two or three of the men he had contacted would agree to come to Takersville to help him take care of Clint Adams.

In his wildest dreams he had not expected all five to agree, but they had.

A chance at the Gunsmith doesn't come around too often, he guessed, and all five men wanted their shot.

So to speak.

Jamie McQuirk felt that the chance to face the Gunsmith was a godsend. Now twenty-nine, he'd been trying for nine years to build himself a reputation, but he knew that he was seen as a second-rater.

If he killed the Gunsmith, however, all that would change.

He left Texas the same day he got the message

from Charlie Taker, with whom he had once ridden when he in his teens.

Oliver "Ollie" Wish was forty-eight. His best days as a gunman were behind him. He knew that. He also knew that a month after he was dead nobody would remember him.

That is, unless he killed—or *was* killed—by the Gunsmith.

He left Arizona the same day he received the message from his old partner, Charlie Taker.

Whitley "Whit" Black was thirty-five. The girl he was in bed with at the moment could have told any-one who was interested that Whit Black was a ladies' man. Women went wide-eyed and weak-kneed when he walked into a room, and wished and hoped for a chance at what he had inside his jeans.

This little lady—a twenty-two-year-old blonde saloon girl—had offered herself to him the minute he had walked into the saloon where she worked in Hamner, New Mexico.

"For free," she'd said, and Whit Black had said, "Come on."

Now she had his penis in her mouth, gobbling it greedily, as he watched the top of her head bob up and down over him. She wasn't real experienced, but her mouth was hot and wet, and he took hold of her head to show her the right tempo.

What the girl couldn't tell anyone—because she didn't know that side of him—was that even better than he liked women, Whit Black liked guns.

He liked carrying them.

He liked cleaning them.

And most of all, he liked using them.

The Takersville Shoot and its grand prize interested him, but the fact that he'd be shooting against the Gunsmith interested him even more. Hell, he didn't even mind the prospect of seeing old Charlie Taker again, after all these years.

As soon as he was finished with whatever-her-name-was—or whenever she was finished with him—he'd mount up and ride for Takersville.

There was money—and a reputation—to be made.

Kenny Last was twenty-two years old, and he thought he was the fastest gun alive. In all of Kenny's practice he concentrated more on speed than accuracy. He felt that if he could get his gun out first, he could take two or three shots before his opponent could fire once.

One of those shots would have to find its mark.

And maybe that mark would be Clint Adams, who had to be as old as the hills, by now.

Or so thought Kenny Last.

He didn't know who Charles Taker was, but the man apparently knew who he was and was giving him a once-in-a-lifetime chance—and offering to pay him, as well!

The fifth man to receive Charles William Taker's message crumpled it up and threw it out.

Reading between the lines—as Taker had naturally intended him to do—he knew that Taker wanted somebody to kill Clint Adams. He also knew that a man like Taker—who he had known very well at one point in both their lives—would not put all of his eggs into one basket. If he sent one telegraph message, then he sent two—or five, or ten.

Clint Adams would be facing as many fast guns as Charles William Taker could find that were willing to face the Gunsmith.

That was a hell of a lot of guns.

The man got up from his hotel room bed, tossed his gear into his saddlebag, and left the room.

From Southern California he could make Takersville, New Mexico, in five days—if he didn't care about killing his horse.

Which he didn't.

Not with what was going on in Takersville.

He wouldn't miss this for the world.

Taker spread the pieces of paper out on his desk and stared at them. He knew four of the five men he'd sent for, and the fifth man was the son of a man he'd known.

It could only have taken a serious threat to him to make him bring them all together in the same town —and *his* town, to boot.

This was going to be like playing with fire—near a keg of gunpowder!

Chapter Seventeen

For the next two days Clint watched Takersville swell to busting with people.

Outside of town, in a clearing, tents were erected for games of chance, corrals for rodeo events, a race track. A medicine wagon arrived, as well as a fortuneteller, and a whore's tent. There was some trouble about the whores with the good women of the town—and with the town whores themselves, who didn't appreciate the competition.

Of the two nights that had passed, Clint had spent one of them with Diane, and one of them alone. He had taken to playing poker in one of the saloons— *not* the one owned by Diehl—until late at night, drinking only an occasional beer. He didn't want his eyes to blur while he was playing cards—or while he was walking back to his hotel. He still had in mind what Diehl and Diane had said about Taker, and he was waiting for such an attempt to either force him from town, injure him, or kill him. None had yet materialized. Maybe Taker was simply going to try to find someone who could beat him.

As confident as Clint Adams was in his own marksmanship, he had never put it to the test against "professional" target-shooters. He had to admit that his interest was piqued.

On the third day, he saw Doc Garfield ride into town. Clint stood on the boardwalk in front of his hotel and watched the older man ride down Main Street, his Sharps carried across his arm. God, Clint thought, he's *aged*. There were lines in his face that he didn't remember, and the hair beneath the hat was gray. He was as big as he'd ever been, and yet he looked as if he'd shrunk some.

Still, it *had* been—what? Three years? Five? When was the last time he saw Doc Garfield?

Hell, he thought, stepping down off the walk, I might as well ask the old buzzard. Maybe he'll remember.

When Clint reached the livery, Doc had already handed his horse over to Diehl and was in the process of trying to chew the liveryman's price down.

"You gotta understand," Diehl said, putting his act on for Doc, "the town's full up. I gotta charge these prices. You won't find cheaper anywhere else."

"Now look, pardner—" Doc began, but Clint interrupted him from behind.

"Stop trying to whittle the man's price down and pay him, you old coot."

Clint saw Doc's shoulders hunch, and he knew the old man had not recognized his voice. Slowly, the man turned, his profile coming into view, and then full face. Just as he recognized Clint, Clint saw that one thing about Doc hadn't changed.

His eyes. They were the same blue that looked like ice when he was angry, and twinkled when he was in a good mood.

They were cold as ice for just the second it took him to recognize Clint, and then they twinkled as the man smiled.

"Well, I'll be—" Doc said.

Clint moved forward and stuck his hand out. The old man took it, and his grip was as dry and firm as ever.

"How the hell are you, Doc?"

"Fine, son, just fine," Doc said. "You're looking the same as always—maybe a little thinner."

"And older?"

"Shoot, son, I ain't the one to go pointing that out about other people."

"Is he a friend of yours, Clint?" Tom Diehl asked, dropping his somewhat dull-witted pretense.

"He sure is, Tom," Clint said. "This is Doc Garfield himself."

"I know who he is," Diehl said, "I just asked if you were friends."

"We're good friends, aren't we, Doc?"

"Well, my memory's been failing me of late, but I seem to recollect that we get along fairly well." Doc turned to Diehl and asked, "What does that entitle me to, friend?"

"The special Clint Adams rate," Diehl said, "and the stall next to that big brute of his."

Doc turned to look at Clint and said, "Is big Duke still hauling that tired, worthless ass of yours around creation?"

"He sure is," Clint said, "and he wouldn't have it any other way."

"Yeah," Doc said, "if he could talk—well shoot, he can nigh onto do everything *but* talk. That critter always was too smart to be stuck with you."

"I guess you're right, Doc. Why don't you pay this man his money and I'll buy you a drink."

"I'll do 'er," Doc said. He turned and paid Tom Diehl the new, reduced "Clint Adams" rate, thanking him for his kindness.

"Now let's get that drink," the old man said. "Seems to me I remember paying for the last *two* drinks . . ."

"What's this about your memory going?" Clint scoffed.

Chapter Eighteen

Clint took Doc Garfield over to the cafe and introduced him to Diane.

"Glad to meet you, Doc. I've heard a lot about you."

"Don't believe a word of it, darlin'," he said.

"It was all good," she insisted.

"Now I *know* it was lies!" he said, and the three of them laughed.

She brought them a pitcher of beer and a couple of bowls of beef stew, then went off to see to the other lunch customers while the two men caught up with each other.

"What's it been, five years, Doc?"

"Seven," he said, "if my memory serves."

Doc finished his first glass of beer in almost one gulp and poured himself a second.

"That sure does cut the dust." He put the pitcher down and looked at Clint. "You ain't here for that contest, are you?"

"I didn't come here for that," Clint said, "but I'm in it, yeah."

Doc frowned.

"You changed your attitude about guns?"

"No."

"Need the money?"

"I can always use money, but no, that's not the reason, either."

"I give up, then," Doc said. "What the hell are you doin' in this contest?"

"A woman," Clint said, because he didn't want to go through the whole series of events.

"Ah," Doc said, "now that's something I can understand. This here Diane the woman?"

"No," Clint said, "not the one I've entered the contest for."

"Uh-huh," Doc said, "but this pretty waitress has been warmin' your bed a bit, huh? Never mind," Doc said, holding up the hand that was holding his fork. "You don't have to answer that. I can tell just by lookin' at her."

"You can, huh?"

"Yep, she's got that look of longing in her eyes."

"You always were a poet, Doc."

"A frontier poet, they call it. That means I ain't got no education."

"Sure you do," Clint said. "A frontier education, they call it."

They finished lunch, talking about old times and old friends—and enemies—and then Clint decided to bring up Charles Taker.

"I understand you shot for Taker one year."

Doc Garfield's face distorted itself into a look of distaste.

"That was a mistake. I figured since he was the organizer and all I'd stand to make a pretty good bundle."

"Didn't you?"

"He tried to hold out on me."

"What happened?"

"I got my money."

"And walked away?"

"Just because he hasn't tried anything yet doesn't mean he won't. That man doesn't forget."

"Why do you keep coming back?"

"To rub his nose in it, I guess. One of these days he'll try to kill me. When he does, I'll be ready." Garfield narrowed his eyes and peered across the table at Clint. "You had a run-in with him?"

Clint nodded.

"He tried to hire me to shoot for him."

"And?"

"I'd already hired on."

"With who?"

"Carol Sydney."

Doc Garfield's eyebrows went up and he whistled appreciatively.

"You know their story?" Clint asked.

"Some," Doc said. "Enough."

"Then you know that information didn't sit well with him."

"Maybe he'll try to kill you."

"Maybe."

"Sounds like we might both need somebody to watch our backs," Doc Garfield said.

"You offering?"

"Sure," Doc said, "are you?"

"I'm game."

"Partners, then?"

"Just long enough to keep each other alive," Clint said, amending the situation, "but when it comes to the shoot—"

"I know," Doc said, holding up his hand, "every man for himself."

Clint found himself staring at Doc Garfield's hand, because it was trembling. Doc seemed to notice and pulled his hand down quickly, but he didn't say anything, so Clint let it lie.

It was then he realized just how *old* Doc Garfield must be. His hand was trembling with *age*!

Clint couldn't help but wonder how his eyes were.

After the meal they walked over to the hotel to get Doc a room.

"I'm sorry," the desk clerk said, shaking his head apologetically "but we filled up very quickly. I'm afraid I have nothing left for Mister Garfield."

Doc turned to Clint and said, "That's all right. I'll see if I can get a place to sleep in the livery or in someone's barn."

"Never mind, Doc," Clint said, putting his hand out to stop him. "You've got a place to sleep."

"Where?"

"My room."

"Won't that be a little cramped?"

"We're partners, aren't we?" Clint said, picking Doc's saddlebags up. "Partners share, don't they?"

"That's right," Doc said, "they do. I'm much obliged, Clint."

"Forget it. Besides, I've got other options open to me, remember?"

"I remember," Doc said, picking up his Sharps, "Just you remember what you said about partners sharing." He was grinning widely.

"Some things you just don't share," Clint said. "Come on, let's get your gear put away in my room."

Chapter Nineteen

Over the next three days people continued to pour into town, which strained at the seams to accommodate them. There were cases where, if you had enough money, a room could be found... somewhere.

A normally quiet town started noisin' up. Men would find themselves an empty space and start practicing their marksmanship at all times of the day, until it was too dark to see. Some of them would take their practice indoors, in which case the sheriff and his deputies had to take action to make sure that target-shooting didn't turn into something else.

Drummers came to town, salesmen hawking their wares on street corners or from wagons. In a meadow outside of town tents started going up and sideshows began. Stock was brought in for the rodeo, and cowpokes started sizing up the opposition.

Takersville was getting ready for the annual rodeo and fair, but most of all, the town was gearing up for this year's Takersville Shoot.

Whit Black was the first man to arrive in response to Taker's telegraph messages. He put his horse up in the livery and went directly to Taker's office, banging on the door hard enough to shake it.

"What the—" he heard someone swear inside. Angry footsteps approached and then the door was flung open. "What the hell—"

Charles Taker stopped short when he saw who was standing in the doorway.

"Whit Black."

"Weren't you expecting me?" Black asked.

"To tell you the truth," Taker said, "I wasn't sure. Come on in."

Taker released the door and walked to his desk. Black entered and closed the door behind him.

"Drink?" Taker asked.

"Whiskey?"

"Brandy."

Black made a face but said, "Why not?"

Taker poured two brandies and handed Black one. The man took it and sat down.

"Is he still here?" he asked.

"He's here," Taker said. "He's entered in the shoot."

"You want him before or after?"

"Can you beat him?"

"That's what we're here to find out, isn't it, Charlie?"

"I mean in the contest. Could you beat him in the contest?"

"You want me to beat him first, and then kill him?"

"If you can," Taker said, "and before he collects his money."

"If he wins."

"Yes, if he wins."

Black frowned and said, "Who else did you send for, Charlie?"

"What makes you think I sent for someone else?"

"You were always one to hedge your bets," Black said. "Who?"

"Ollie Wish, Jamie McQuirk, Kenny Last, a few others."

"Anyone else here yet?"

"No," Taker said, "but then I figured if you did come, you'd be the first to arrive. Where did my message find you?"

"Here in New Mexico, in a town called Hamner."

"I don't know it."

"Well, it ain't much, but its got a telegraph office, a saloon, and a whorehouse."

"All the comforts of home, huh?"

"Good enough. What does it mean that I got here first?" Black asked.

"I want you to ride herd on the others."

"Are they gonna enter the contest?"

"If they want."

"And do we all take turns at Adams afterward? Or do we draw straws?"

"You'll all get paid, no matter who kills him. It doesn't matter to me who does it."

"It'll matter to them," Black said, "and it matters to me."

"Well, you'll be in charge, Whit," Taker said. "Set it up so you get the first shot."

Black frowned.

"I know Ollie and Jamie—who's this Kenny Last?"

"A kid—like Jamie was a kid when we met him."

"That ain't sayin' much." Black drank his brandy,

looked around the office and then got up and walked to the window. Taker swiveled his chair around to watch him.

"You got a nice setup here," Black said.

"I like it."

"The whole town yours?"

"Just about."

"Real nice," Black said. He turned and looked at Taker. "How bad you want this Gunsmith?"

"Pretty bad," Taker said, after a moment. "There's a piece of land I want, and I'm close to getting it. He could get in my way." Taker didn't bother telling Black about Carol Sydney and Clint.

"I remember what you used to do to people who got in your way, Charlie."

"I still do it."

"Why don't you take care of this yourself, Charlie?" Black asked.

"Because I don't do my own dirty work anymore, Whit," Taker said. "I have it done for me."

Whit Black turned away from the window and looked at Charles Taker.

"Like hiring me?"

Taker stared back at him.

"Just like hiring you."

Black stared hard at Taker for a few moments, and when the other man didn't avert his eyes he said, "You're still a bastard, ain't you, Charlie?"

"You don't seem to have changed much either, Whit," Taker said.

"A little, maybe," Black said, "but not a whole lot, no."

"What do you say, Whit?" Taker asked. "Are you working for me?"

Black looked down at the remainder of the brandy in his glass, made a face, and put it down on the desk.

"If you've got some whiskey around here someplace, I'm working for you."

Taker nodded and said, "I think I can take care of that."

Chapter Twenty

Whit Black was there to meet each of the others as they arrived.

Ollie Wish rode into Takersville and marveled at how busy the place was. He had ridden past the meadow on his way in, which was already alive and teeming with people looking for some way to either spend their money or lose it. A game of chance, or a fortune told, the money went just the same.

Wish put his horse in the livery and asked the liveryman where he could find Charles Taker. After receiving directions to Taker's building, he went there. He saw the name stenciled on the big window on the second floor, but even before he got to the stairway he saw Whitley Black sitting at a desk downstairs as he entered.

"Whit?"

"Hello, Ollie."

"Charlie sent for you, too?"

"And some others."

"Why?"

"Hedging his bets, as usual."

"He hasn't changed?" Ollie Wish asked.

"He's a lot richer," Black said, "but other than that he hasn't changed."

"I'll go up and—"

"There's no need for you to talk to him," Black said. "I'm in charge."

"Of what?"

Black smiled.

"Let me tell you about that," Black said, "and then there's something else very important we have to talk about."

"Like what?"

"Like our futures."

Jamie McQuirk was the next to arrive, and followed basically the same course taken by Ollie Wish the day before, except that McQuirk stopped at the saloon first for a beer.

After that he went and found Whit Black waiting for him, to discuss his future.

When Kenny Last rode in, he exhibited the impatience of youth and went straight to Taker's office, asking someone on the street where it was.

He found Whit Black, Ollie Wish, and Jamie McQuirk. He didn't know any of them, but once that was remedied, Whit Black asked Kenny a question.

"I know you're young, boy," he said, "but have you thought about your future?"

"Not a whole lot," Kenny admitted.

"Let me tell you a story, son . . ." Whit Black said.

The fifth man who received Taker's telegraph message, with no intentions of responding to it, rode into town the day before the fair, rodeo, and shoot were all to start. (In point of fact that "fair" had begun already in the meadow, but it wasn't officially set to start until the following day.)

He left his horse at the livery and then went looking for a hotel room. When he had no luck, he went back to the livery and asked the man how much he wanted to let him sleep in a stall.

"I don't have an empty stall, friend," Tom Diehl told him, "but you're welcome to make yourself a hay bed anywhere there's room."

"Thank you," the man said. "Tell me, do you know Charles Taker?"

A look of distaste came over the liveryman's face and he admitted, "Yes, I know him."

"He own this town?"

"Pretty much," Diehl said, "but there's parts he doesn't."

"Like this one?"

"Like this one."

The man smiled and said, "I thought as much."

"Why's that?"

"The look on your face when I said his name."

"It showed?" Diehl said. "I've got to watch that."

"I won't tell anyone," the man assured him. "I'll go and make that hay bed, in case you offer space to anyone else."

"I'm not that generous, friend."

"Then why me?"

"Don't know yet," Diehl said. "I expect I'll find an answer before you leave."

"I expect you will," the man said. "Tell me something else."

"What?"

"That big black gelding I can see from here. He belong to the Gunsmith?"

Diehl frowned and asked, "Why do you want to know that?"

"Just want to know if I recognize the horse."

"You do," Diehl said. "You know the horse, you know the rider, too?"

"Some," the man said. "Some. I'll take care of that hay bed."

He walked past Diehl into the livery, leaving the liveryman to scratch his head.

He had a feeling about the man.

He hoped he wouldn't turn out to be wrong.

Chapter Twenty-One

The day the whole shebang got started, Clint woke up in Diane's bed. She was tucked warmly against him and he could feel her breath on his back. He'd been spending his nights with her since moving Doc Garfield into his room, and she had assured him that she wouldn't see that as a desire on his part to set up anything permanent.

"That's good," Clint said, "because I'm just trying to get away from Doc's snoring."

Now he lay still, waiting to see if she would shift position without him having to move and wake her . . .

Yesterday he had signed up for the shoot and had lingered to see if he could recognize some of the other contestants.

"You won't see too many familiar faces, Clint," Doc Garfield said.

"Why's that?"

"Because it's a different world. A lot of these guys are great shots, but they won't go into a saloon because they don't have the guts. Their style is shooting at glass balls and cardboard targets."

"What are you doing here, then?"

"Good question," Doc said. "I started competing about fifteen years ago. There's good money in this if you compete enough, and if you win enough. There are no more buffalo, and I just can't see myself turning bounty hunter. Being a lawman just doesn't pay enough." Doc shrugged and said, "What else is there for me to do?"

Clint wondered what Doc Garfield would do when the shaking of his hands got worse, or when his eyesight failed him—if it hadn't already.

Doc had been right. Clint didn't recognize any of the other contestants, but he left the saloon where the signing was being held before the last of the contestants signed their names, or he might have recognized the very last man to sign up . . .

Now he decided he couldn't wait much longer and started to move his leg. She sensed the move and encircled him with her arm. There would be no way he could move now without waking her, so he decided to wake her up the best way he knew how.

He turned over quickly and leaned into her so that he could lick her breasts. She moaned when his tongue came into contact with her nipples, and dug her nails into his back.

"Are you trying to tell me something?" she asked, lazily.

"Yes," he said, "it's time for one of us to get up."

"Well, it isn't me," she said.

"Mmm," he said, biting her right nipple and sliding his hand between her legs, "I'm starting to think it isn't me, either."

She reached between them and took hold of his

penis which was hard, and said, "I know it isn't you."

She slid down so that she could lick the length of him, and then take him into her mouth.

It was a little while before he finally did get up . . .

As it turned out, Diane rose with him, and they went down to the hotel dining room for breakfast. It was early enough that there were still tables available. With the population of the town having nearly doubled, at a time when the dining room was usually empty it looked like it was the middle of the morning, instead of very early.

While they were having breakfast, they saw Doc Garfield enter the dining room. At this time there were no tables available, so Clint waved Doc to their table.

"This is ridiculous," Doc said, sitting down. "They should make sure people who are actually guests of the hotel get served first."

"That would leave you out," Clint pointed out, and Doc gave him a look.

"Well, I'll leave you men to your talk," Diane said, standing up.

"You're not leaving on my account, are you?" Doc asked.

"I'm leaving so my cafe can get some of this business," she said. "I guess I'm not a very good businesswoman, taking care of my own breakfast first."

"There's plenty of business to go around, Diane," Clint said. "This town is ready to explode."

"I'll see you later," she said to Clint. He was glad she didn't lean over and give him a wifely peck on the cheek or lips. "Enjoy your breakfast," she said to Doc.

"If I was worried about enjoying my breakfast I'd come with you and eat your cooking," Doc said.

"You're sweet."

As she left, Doc said, "That's a sweet little gal."

"Yes, she is."

"You ain't gettin' serious about her, are you?"

"No," Clint said, without hesitation.

"Good. I ain't never got serious about a woman in my life."

A waiter came over and Doc ordered breakfast. Clint told the man to bring a fresh pot of coffee.

"So, the whole to-do starts today, huh?" Doc said.

"I guess so. When do you shoot?"

"At noon."

"I shoot at one, immediately following you."

"Are you using your handgun?"

"Only if I want to win," Clint said.

"Your handgun against my Sharps, huh?"

"Well, let's not say it's between the two of us, Doc," Clint said. "You know these fellas better than I do. Who's going to be the most troublesome?"

"Whit Black is here, and I'm surprised about that," Doc said. "He doesn't usually shoot in competition."

"Wait a minute," Clint said, "I know that name."

"Sure, just like you know the name Ollie Wish."

"Wish is here, too?"

Doc nodded, and sat back as the waiter arrived with his eggs.

"Whit Black and Ollie Wish," Clint said. "What are they doing here?"

"Maybe they're not here for the contest," Doc said. "Maybe they're here for you."

"Or you."

"Either one is possible."

"Who else is here?"

Doc reeled off a few other names of regular contest competitors whom Clint did not know.

"And there are the unknown factors," Doc said. "There were quite a few people signing up that I don't know."

"Cowpokes."

"Maybe, but one of those cowpokes could up and surprise everyone."

"I suppose so."

"After breakfast you wanna go and watch some of the rodeo? Maybe see some of the fair?"

"Why not?" Clint said. "What else is there to do?"

When Carol Sydney woke up that morning, she felt anything but rested. The muscles in her neck and shoulders were knotted, and she felt as if she had been up all night.

Today was the day the shoot started, and she hadn't talked to Clint Adams since that night at her house. Was he still intending to represent her? Or had he been bought off by Taker by this time?

The only way she was going to know anything was to ride into town and attend the fair and rodeo. Around noon, when the shoot was scheduled to begin, was when she'd find out if Clint was indeed going to shoot for her.

She dressed quickly and went out to get someone to saddle her horse. Most of the men had already left to go to town, as she had given them the day off to attend the first day of the festivities. The rest of the week only the men competing in any of the events would be allowed to leave the ranch.

She went to the livery, and saddled her own horse, and rode to town.

Whit Black, Ollie Wish, Jamie McQuirk, and Kenny Last had all been given rooms by Charles Taker in one of the buildings he owned. Now they were all gathered in Black's room.

"All right, you've all heard my idea," Black said. "What do you think?"

He looked at Ollie Wish first, because Wish was the oldest and the others knew who he was. Black felt that if Wish went along with him, the others would, also.

"What you're talking about is double-crossing Charlie Taker," Wish said.

"So?" Black asked. "Is there a man here who hasn't been double-crossed one time or another?"

"Not by Taker," Kenny Last said.

"Son, you ain't old enough to answer that question," Black said. "You didn't know Charlie Taker before he became rich. He'd do anything to make himself some money, and that included stealing from his partners."

"He stole from you?" Kenny asked.

"That was a long time ago," Ollie Wish said.

"Some people have short memories," Whit Black said, staring at Ollie Wish.

"I remember, Whit," Wish said.

"Then what do you say, Ollie? Are you with me on this or not?"

Wish took a moment, then nodded, and said, "All

right, damn it. I'm too old to start having scruples now. I'm with you."

"And you two?"

"I'm in," Jamie McQuirk said. "I don't owe Charlie nothing."

"Kid?"

Kenny Last stared at Whit Black. He hated it when Black called him "kid," and that decided him as much as anything else. He was going to show Whit Black that he wasn't no kid.

"I'm in," he said.

"All right," Black said, "there's one other thing we've got to talk about."

"What's that?" Kenny Last asked.

"Clint Adams," Ollie Wish said, and Black nodded.

"The Gunsmith," Black said. "We're all here because of a chance at him, right?"

"That's right," Jamie McQuirk said.

"So, do we forget about him or do we try for him before we make our move?"

"If one of us kills him," Ollie Wish said, "everyone gets paid, right?"

"Right," Black said.

"And then we can make our move *after* we get paid."

"Right again."

"So I guess the question is," Ollie Wish said, "who gets to try him?"

"We'll draw straws," Black said, "unless somebody disagrees."

They all exchanged glances and no one objected.

"And there's something else," Ollie Wish said.

"What?" Black asked.

"Charlie," Ollie said. "How do you think he's going to react when he finds out what we done?"

"Then maybe we ought to take care of him, too, before we leave," Jamie McQuirk said.

"We'll talk about that later," Black said. "I have some thoughts on that, but I want to wait a while before we talk about them. Right now, let's draw those straws and see who gets to kill the Gunsmith."

Chapter Twenty-Two

Clint and Doc spent the morning watching the rodeo events, and Clint noticed that Carol's ranch hands seemed to be doing fairly well.

At one point during the morning Clint looked across one of the corrals that had been erected for the purpose of the rodeo, and saw Carol standing on the other side, talking to her foreman.

"That is a fine-lookin' woman," Doc Garfield said.

"That she is."

At that point Carol looked up and saw Clint looking at her.

"Somethin's flashin' through the air, here," Doc said. "What's goin' on?"

"We had a difference of opinion not long ago," Clint replied. "I guess neither one of us has recovered from it, yet."

"You still gonna shoot for her?"

"I made a promise."

"Think maybe you oughta tell her that?"

"Maybe you're right."

Clint pushed away from the corral and started walking around. Carol saw him, but stood her ground and waited for him.

"Hello," he said.

"I was looking for you earlier," she said.

"Oh?"

"I wanted to make sure we still have a deal."

"I said we did," he said. "I stand by my word."

"So do I," she said. "What time do you shoot?"

"One."

"I'll see you then."

She turned to walk away, and as he started after her, the foreman, Bill Wren, stepped in front of him.

"The lady don't want to talk to you no more."

"Move out of my way, friend."

Wren, who was just about an inch shorter than Clint, matched stares with Clint until Carol Sydney showed up at his shoulder and said, "Stop acting like an ass, Wren."

Instantly deflated, he averted his eyes and moved out of Clint's way.

Carol stared at Clint and said, "I don't think we have anything to say to each other until after the contest is over."

"If that's the way you want it," Clint said, and turned and walked away.

Carol stared after him for a moment, then turned to watch one of her men get thrown from a horse.

Charles William Taker loved looking out his window. That was because he owned almost everything he could see. It was a special feeling he got when he looked down at it all. He had become a fixture in that window. People walking on the streets knew that, nine times out of ten, if they lifted their heads and looked up there they'd see him, looking down on them.

Right now, however, the town looked deserted. He knew everyone was out in the meadow—which was land he also owned—watching all of the contests.

The shoot wouldn't start until twelve, and he had four men entered. Out of Black, Wish, McQuirk, and Last he thought that Black had the best chance of beating Clint Adams. He would be the one who would be least intimidated by the man's reputation.

Ollie Wish had a chance, too, only because he was too old to care if he lost. There'd be no pressure on him when he shot.

McQuirk and Last were under thirty, and young enough that they'd be hit by nerves as well as bravado. Neither of them had a shot at beating him.

Taker looked at his watch and saw that it was twenty minutes to twelve. He took his jacket off the back of his chair and slipped it on.

Even if Clint Adams won, he'd find out that he was a loser.

As Taker walked through town to the meadow, he thought about the four men who had responded to his telegraph messages. He knew he couldn't trust any of them, no matter how much he offered to pay them, and they probably felt they couldn't trust him. He knew that once they had killed Clint Adams for him, they'd probably try to double-cross him in some way. If they did, it would be Whit Black's idea. Black had never forgiven him for an incident that took place ten years earlier. They had robbed a bank and made a much larger haul than they had thought. Taker couldn't help himself. At his first opportunity he had taken all of the money and left Black behind. Later —months later—he had found Black and sent him some money, because using the money he'd stolen he had already begun to make his fortune. He was sure that the gesture had not appeased Black at all.

Black hadn't mentioned the incident, but Taker knew the man would never forget.

So, if there was a double-cross in the works, it would be engineered by Whit Black.

Surely Black didn't think that would come as a surprise to Taker?

Did he?

The fifth man was still pretty much unnoticed by the others. He had purposely arrived late to sign up for the shoot. As far as he knew there were only two people in town who would recognize him—Clint Adams and Charles Taker—and neither was there when he signed up. If one of them looked at the list of contestants, of course, they'd recognize the name, but there wasn't any reason for either of them to do that.

The first time they'd see him would be at the contest, and he was still trying to decide what he would say to each of them.

Chapter Twenty-Three

Clint Adams was amazed by Doc Garfield.

When the man held a glass, or a fork, or tried to roll a cigarette, his hands shook.

When he held that big Sharps in his hands, he was rock steady.

The first round of shooting involved stationary targets with conventional bull's-eyes. Doc fired twenty shots, and every one was in the black bull's-eye.

Also shooting were Whit Black, Ollie Wish, and a fella named K.C. Burke. Those fellas also hit the black on every shot.

Of the ten people shooting, those four advanced to the next round.

"Nice shooting, Doc," Clint said.

"This stationary stuff is a breeze," Doc said. "Wait until they get to the moving targets. Good luck."

"Thanks."

"Not that you need it."

"You always need luck, Doc."

Clint lined up with nine other shooters. Down the line from him were Kenny Last and Jamie McQuirk. They and Clint were the only three shooting with handguns. The rest were firing with rifles.

On the line Clint recognized two men from Carol's ranch, including the foreman, Bill Wren.

"Fire when ready!" a man called out. "Twenty shots, at your own pace."

Clint fired his twenty shots, all in the black, and finished well before anyone else. He stepped away from the line while a judge waited for the others to finish before he checked Clint's target.

"Very impressive," Doc said, grinning.

"Like you said, a stationary target is no challenge," Clint said, ejecting the spent shells and reloading.

He turned and watched as the others finished their shooting. Beyond them he could see Carol Sydney, who had a smile on her face. Was it because he had fired twenty shots straight and true? Or had someone from her ranch done the same?

The others had completed their firing now, and the judges went to the targets and began waving to the main judge.

All of the shooters had numbers on their backs. Clint's number was 7, and that was the first number the main judge called out as having shot a perfect round.

"Congratulations," Doc said, unnecessarily.

Clint looked over at Carol, and she was smiling even wider.

All in all, four of the shooters—including Clint— had fired perfect rounds and would advance to the next. Bill Wren, Carol's foreman, was one of them. Clint didn't know who the other men were.

Kenny Last and Jamie McQuirk were not among

the four. Kenny Last had two misses, Jamie McQuirk three, and neither man was happy.

"Congratulations," Clint heard someone say, and it wasn't Doc Garfield. He turned and saw Charles Taker.

"To both of you," Taker said, including Doc. "That was some fine shooting."

Doc turned and walked away from Taker.

"It doesn't look like Doc likes you, Taker," Clint said.

"And you, Adams? I don't see you turning your back on me."

"Oh, I don't like you any more than he does, Taker. I'm just more polite about it."

"I see Carol Sydney looks happy."

"She should. Her foreman shot a perfect round."

"Wren?" Taker said, making a face. "He's no marksman. A stationary target offers no challenge to anyone. He'll never make it through the next round. No, she must be smiling because of your round. That was very impressive, by the way. Why haven't you ever competed before?"

"I don't feel that guns are anything to play with, Taker," Clint said. "That's what all of these people are doing, playing games with instruments of death."

"That's a very dramatic stance, Adams, but I don't know that you'd find very many people here who would agree with you."

"That doesn't matter, Taker," Clint said. "My opinions are my own, and not influenced by what anyone else says or thinks."

People were moving around them, as men moved to take up their position for the next round.

"Excuse me," Clint said, "I want to make room for the next round."

Clint walked away from Taker to find a position from which he could watch the third round of shooting.

It wasn't until the final round of shooting—the last nine of one hundred and nine competitors—that the fifth recipient of one of Taker's telegraph messages stepped up to the line, and was seen by both Taker and Clint Adams.

"I don't believe it," Clint said.

"What don't you believe?" Doc Garfield asked.

"Do you see the man in the center?"

"The man in the—you mean the black one?"

"Yes, the black one."

"You know him?"

"I know him real well," Clint said. "His name is Fred Hammer."

"I've heard of him," Garfield said. "Don't they call him something ridiculous like the Black Gun?"

"They do."

"I've never heard of him competing before."

"Neither have I."

"This should be interesting, then."

"Maybe," Clint said, "it just might be."

Taker saw the black man standing in the center of the line and stared. He wondered why—if Fred Hammer was in Takersville—he hadn't come to see him. Was he there in response to his message, or was it just a coincidence? He'd never competed in the Takersville Shoot before, so why was he there now?

That was something he was going to find out.

Fred Hammer was using his handgun and fired all twenty shots right into the black.

Hammer was a tall man, almost six four, with wide shoulders and a powerful chest. He and Clint Adams had met sometime ago, and while they weren't exactly friends, they did respect each other.[1]

Hammer was the first to complete his twenty shots, and as he holstered his gun, he looked over at Clint Adams and smiled.

"Son of a bitch," Clint said as Hammer approached him.

"You or me?" Hammer said.

"What the hell are you doing here?"

"I just happened to be in the neighborhood."

The two men shook hands and then Clint introduced Hammer to Garfield.

"This is a real pleasure," Hammer said. "I've heard about you for a long time, Doc."

"Well, I've heard of you, too, Fred."

"Now that we've got that bullshit out of the way," Clint said, "why don't we go and get a drink?"

"Lead the way," Hammer said. "You know this town better than I do."

"How long have you been here?" Clint asked.

"Since yesterday."

"Then you're right," Clint said. "Follow me."

Charles William Taker watched Fred Hammer and Clint Adams shake hands, and frowned. They greeted each other like they were—if not old friends—old acquaintances. He watched them walk away

---

[1] *The Gunsmith #28*

with Doc Garfield, and he wondered how well these three men really knew each other, and how much of a coincidence their meeting here really was.

And then he wondered if he'd sent for enough men to do the job on Clint Adams, after all.

"Do you see what I see?" Ollie Wish asked Whit Black.

"I see it," Black said. "Adams, Doc Garfield, and a big black dude."

"That big black," Ollie Wish said, "is Fred Hammer. You've heard of Hammer, haven't you?"

"Fred Hammer?" Black said. "What the hell is he doing here? And what's he doing with Adams and Garfield?"

"Could Taker have sent for him?"

"He might have," Black said. "Maybe we'd better find out, so that we know whose side he's on."

"And how many guns we're supposed to go up against," Wish said. "I'll tell you right now, I won't be comfortable facing Adams *and* Hammer with only Last and McQuirk to back us up."

"I agree," Black said, "but let's see what we can find out first."

Chapter Twenty-Four

Clint took both Hammer and Garfield to the saloon secretly owned by Tom Diehl. The town was almost deserted, and when they entered the saloon, the only person there was the bartender.

Clint went to the bar to get three beers and carried them to a table where Hammer and Garfield were already seated. When Doc Garfield picked up his beer, his hand shook noticeably, and Clint saw Hammer look his way quickly.

"That's good," Doc said, putting the mug down half empty.

Hammer drank some, and Clint sipped his.

"What are you doing here, Fred?" Clint asked. "I can't believe you came here to compete in the Great Takersville Shoot."

"I could say the same thing about you, Clint," Fred Hammer said. "What are you doing shooting in a contest like this?"

"A woman," Doc Garfield said.

Hammer nodded and said, "That explains it."

"That *doesn't* explain it," Clint said, and launched into his story for Hammer's benefit.

When he was finished, Doc Garfield said, "That's what I said, a woman."

"I think I saw her," Hammer said. "Tall woman, wide shoulders, good—"

"That's her," Clint said.

"Well, then, I can understand it."

"Now it's your turn."

Hammer took a drink from his mug first.

"I got a telegraph message from Charlie Taker."

"Taker?" Clint said. "Do you know him?"

"We did some business over the years, before he became so rich," Hammer said.

"Why did he send you a message now?"

"He asked me to come to town, and told me that you were here," Hammer said.

"He didn't say why he wanted you?"

"No, but that's not hard to figure, is it?"

"To shoot against me in the contest?"

"Possibly," Hammer said. "Have you gotten in his way?"

"I have."

"Then he may want me to get you out of his way."

"Are you for hire for that purpose?"

"Not necessarily," Hammer said. "I got here yesterday, but I haven't been to see him yet. There's another thing to consider, though."

"What?"

"I can't believe that I'm the only one he contacted," Hammer said. "There have to be some other fellas in town who may already be working for him."

"Did you recognize anyone?"

"Nobody that I knew when I knew him," Hammer said, "but Charlie Taker has a wide and varied background, Clint. In fact, I'm surprised he doesn't enter the contest and shoot for himself."

"He's good?" Clint asked.

"He was *very* good, at one time."

Clint looked at Doc Garfield and asked, "Did you know that?"

"No, I never heard that."

"And not all of his money has been made legally."

"I'd heard that," Garfield said.

"There aren't too many businessmen who *have* made their fortunes honestly, or legally."

"No, I'm talking about *before* he made his fortune. Taker hit his share of banks and trains when he was younger."

Clint looked at Doc again who said, "I hadn't heard that, either."

"He keeps it pretty quiet," Hammer said.

"How did you get to know him?"

"We did some jobs together," Hammer said, "when I was younger."

"This man is becoming more and more interesting," Clint said.

"He was always a dangerous man, Clint," Hammer said, "and more than a little treacherous. He wasn't beyond stealing from his partners. I don't know how much he's changed, but I'd operate under the assumption that he was still dangerous."

"I believe he is," Clint said, "only he now has enough money to have other people do his dirty work for him."

"Like me," Hammer said.

"Like you, and whoever these other fellas are."

"If there are others," Garfield said.

"Oh, there are others," Hammer said. "You can count on it."

"I guess I'd better try to find out who they are, and how many there are," Clint said.

"Well, if I can help you do that . . ." Hammer said.

"Do you think you might want to talk to Taker first?" Clint asked. "Maybe listen to what he has to offer?"

Hammer fiddled with his mug and said, "That might be a good idea. Who knows, maybe he'll offer me enough money to compromise my principles."

"I didn't know you had any," Clint said.

Hammer grinned and said, "Neither does Taker."

Chapter Twenty-Five

"You said you sent for some people who didn't come," Whit Black said to Charles Taker. "Was Fred Hammer one of those?"

Black and Wish had confronted Taker, and he had insisted that they wait until they were in his office before they discussed anything.

As they entered the office, Black could see that Taker wasn't happy to have Ollie Wish present, so Black made a show of asking Wish to wait outside. Wish, understanding, agreed and left the room.

"I did send a message to Hammer, yes," Taker admitted.

"How well do you know him?"

"About as well as any of you. We worked together years ago."

"So he may be a different man than the one you knew years ago."

Taker looked at Black and said, "How different are you and I, Whit?"

"Some people change, Charlie," Black said. "How come he didn't stop in to see you?"

"Maybe he just got in today."

"He had to be here yesterday to sign up for the contest," Black pointed out.

"That's right."

"If he's going to be siding with Adams, we're going to need some help."

"Maybe we'd better find out what he's doing here before we start to panic," Taker said.

"I'm not panicking," Black said. "I can count on Ollie Wish in any situation, but those are other two: I don't think you showed any real great judgment in sending for them."

"McQuirk does what he's told."

"He's too young, and what does that say for Kenny Last? I don't know *what* to expect from him."

"I'll talk to Hammer and find out what's going on," Taker said, "and then we'll talk again."

"You'll go to him, then?"

"No," Taker said, "I think he'll come here. He's got to listen to my offer, otherwise why did he come all this way? Not to compete, that's for sure."

"All right," Black said, "you talk to Hammer and let me know what he says. I know of a few good boys I can get here within the next couple of days."

"Who?"

"Nobody you know," Black said, "but boys that I can trust."

"But can I trust them?"

"You're paying me," Black said, "and they'll do what I tell them." Black moved to the door and said, "Let me know as soon as you talk to Hammer."

"You'll be the first to know, Whit."

After Black left, Taker frowned. He didn't appreciate the fact that Black wanted to bring in his own men, whom *he* could trust.

I don't trust you, Whit, Taker thought. How could I trust any men that you bring in?

Taker knew a man he could have in town within the next two days, also, only he was *very* expensive. Alone he'd cost more than Black, Wish, McQuirk, and Last.

Maybe it was time to bring him into this—which Taker should probably have done in the first place.

Chapter Twenty-Six

If most of the town hadn't been out in the meadow, watching rodeo action, or sideshows, the big black man would have attracted a lot more attention than he did walking down the street. His stride was purposeful and long and—physically speaking —he was as perfect a specimen as any woman could want.

Men would have noticed him because he had the look of a man whose way you'd want to get out of.

Fred Hammer had learned long ago that white folks were intimidated by him not *because* he was black, but because he didn't seem to notice that he was black.

Hammer saw Taker's window before he reached the building and saw two men coming out. He recognized them as shooters from the contest. They didn't notice him because they turned the other way as they exited and started off down the street.

Hammer entered the building, went upstairs, and knocked on the door to Taker's office.

When Taker opened the door, he was surprised to see Hammer standing there.

"Hello, Fred."

"Charlie."

"Come on in."

Hammer entered and closed the door. Taker went around behind his desk and didn't offer Hammer a drink.

"I was a little surprised to see you this afternoon," Taker said. "I was also surprised that you hadn't come to see me."

"I'm here now, aren't I?"

"Sure," Taker said, "sure you're here, now that you've talked to Adams."

"What's that got to do with anything?"

"You and Adams go back a ways?"

"Not as far back as we go, Charlie," Hammer said. "You sure have come up in the world, haven't you?"

"You haven't done so badly, Fred."

"I'm not rich."

"You're respected," Taker said. "If I remembered correctly, I *wanted* to be rich, and you *wanted* to be respected. I guess we both got what we wanted, eh?"

"I guess so, Charlie. Tell me, why did you ask me to come here?"

"I just thought you might be interested in our little contest."

Taker wasn't about to tell Hammer the real reason he'd sent for him, not until he knew what the man had in mind.

Hammer wasn't about to believe a bald-faced lie like that, but he realized that Taker was being careful with him since he had obviously seen him with Clint Adams.

"We going to dance around each other, Charlie?" Hammer asked.

"You tell me, Fred," Taker said. "Why did you come to town?"

"To see what you wanted."

"Why didn't you come and see me as soon as you got here?"

"I wasn't aware that was a requirement," Hammer said. "I got in yesterday afternoon, took a look at the town, signed up for the contest, found someplace to sleep . . . and that wasn't easy."

"If you'd come to see me, you'd have a room right now. What do you have now, a bed of hay somewhere?"

"It's comfortable enough."

"It better be," Taker said, "because that's where you're staying."

"Why's that?"

"I can't trust you, Fred."

Hammer smiled, his teeth shining.

"I *never* could trust you, Charlie."

"The difference is, you always knew that. This is a new Hammer I'm seeing."

"How so?"

"What if I told you I asked you here to hire you to kill a man?"

"I don't hire my gun out for murder, Charlie."

"See? A new Hammer."

"Not so new," Hammer said. "I was never for hire as a killer."

"I've seen you kill your fair share."

"For the same reasons you did, to protect myself."

"I've followed your career, you know."

"Not much of a career."

"You've got a reputation as a good hand with a gun."

"Lots of folks do. You did, at one time. Can you still shoot?"

"I don't have to, anymore," Taker said. "I hire it done, Hammer."

"Is that what you wanted me for?"

"I had a proposition for you, but I don't think I'll give it to you, now."

"You mean I made this trip for nothing?"

"No, you made it for a reason," Taker said, "I just don't have any idea what that reason could be, and that bothers me."

"I saw two men leaving when I got here," Hammer said. "They working for you?"

"You're not working for me," Taker said, "so I'm not going to talk to you about who is."

"What's the big secret, Charlie?"

"If I told you, it wouldn't be a secret."

"How much you paying?"

"Why? Money make you change your mind?"

"It might."

Taker studied Hammer for a few moments.

"You don't have that look in your eyes anymore, Hammer."

"What look is that?"

"The one I always remember seeing," Taker said. "The hard look that said to hell with everybody else, you were going to do what was good for you no matter what."

"I still do what's good for me."

"But the 'no matter what' is gone, isn't it?"

"I'm getting tired of this, Charlie," Hammer said. "If you don't want me to work for you, just say so."

"I don't want you to work for me."

"I'll need a kill fee."

"A what?"

"A kill fee," Hammer said. "I came here because I thought you had a deal for me. You've killed that deal. I need to be compensated for my trouble."

"Compensated—"

"Don't make me ask again, Charlie," Hammer said. "I need my expenses covered."

"Are you holding me up, Hammer?"

"That's not how I see it."

"I don't have a gun on."

"What's that got to do with anything?"

"Just in case you had an idea of robbing me—"

"I'm not robbing you, Charlie," Hammer said. "I'm asking you to pay my expenses."

Taker studied Hammer and then opened a drawer. He took some money out, then took out an envelope and put the money into it. He closed the drawer and handed Hammer the envelope.

"Don't count it here," Taker said. "If you don't think it's enough I'm not inclined to give you any more."

Hammer took the envelope and moved toward the door.

"I'm sorry we can't do business, Charlie," Hammer said.

"Hammer?"

"Yeah?"

"Don't get in my way."

"I don't even know where your way is, Charlie."

"Everywhere," Taker said. "This is my town, and while you're here, you're liable to get in my way."

"If that's the case," Hammer said, "then you'd have to move me out of your way, wouldn't you?"

"I never liked you, Hammer," Taker said. "It

wouldn't bother me if I had to move you."

"I just hope you try it yourself, Charlie."

Taker smiled. "Just because I'm not wearing a gun now doesn't mean I don't still know how to use one."

"I guess I'd have to see that for myself, wouldn't I, Charlie?"

"Ah, I already told you, Hammer, I don't have to do it myself anymore."

"Then hire yourself somebody good."

"Don't take sides, Hammer," Taker said. "It wouldn't be healthy."

Hammer raised the hand holding the envelope, then decided not to say anything else. All they were doing was fencing, and he was never much good at that.

Hammer went outside and cursed himself. He'd blown it. What he had wanted was for Taker to tell him Yeah, he wanted to hire him to take the Gunsmith out of his way. What he'd gotten was nothing except an envelope with some money in it, and by forcing that out of Taker—something he'd done just for the perverse pleasure of it—he had probably put himself right at the top of Charlie Taker's list.

After Hammer left, Charlie Taker stood up and went to the window. He watched the big black man walk away until he was out of sight, and then left his office himself.

He had to go to the sheriff's office and report a robbery.

Chapter Twenty-Seven

"I let my dislike for the man get the better of me," Hammer explained to Clint.

Clint and Doc Garfield had waited at the saloon for Hammer to come back, and as soon as the man walked through the door they knew that something had gone wrong.

"It was crazy," Hammer said. "I haven't even seen him for years and yet as soon as I saw him, that old feeling of . . . of intense dislike—maybe even hatred—rose up in me again. We started fencing back and forth with words, and I *hate* that."

"So you didn't get anything out of him?" Garfield asked.

"Some veiled threats, but they were only directed at me," Hammer said. "Oh, and I got this."

He put the envelope on the table.

"What's that?" Clint asked.

"I told him I wanted him to cover my expenses for the trip here."

"And he paid?" Clint asked.

"Well, I had a gun and he didn't."

"That sounds like robbery," Garfield said.

"No," Hammer said, shaking his head, "he'd never make that claim stick."

"He would if he owned the sheriff," Garfield said.

"And he does," Clint said.

All three men exchanged glances.

"No wonder he paid up so willingly," Hammer said. "He's going to set me up."

"How much is in there?" Clint asked.

"I haven't counted it."

Clint opened the envelope and counted out two hundred and fifty dollars.

"Shit, I'm worth more than that."

"This is just enough to make it look good," Clint said, putting the money back in the envelope. "You can't walk around with this on you, Hammer."

"What do you suggest I do with it?"

"Let one of us carry it, for now. If he's trying to set you up, he'll have the sheriff looking for you by now. When he doesn't find the money on you, he'll have to let you go for lack of evidence."

"Not if he owns the sheriff like you say," Garfield said. "The sheriff will take his word for it that Hammer robbed him."

"His word won't be worth much," Clint said, "against ours." He looked at Hammer and said, "We'll swear that you were here with us all afternoon, and that you didn't go anywhere near Taker's office. The sheriff'll have to let you go or let that come out in front of a judge."

"Sounds good to me," Hammer said. "I'm not about to let some crooked lawman put me behind bars."

"Did anyone else see you go into Taker's office?"

"No, nobody saw me," Hammer said, "but I saw a couple of people. Two fellas who were shooters at the contest."

He described them and Garfield nodded saying, "Whit Black and Ollie Wish."

"I know those names," Hammer said. "Those fellas don't travel around entering contests."

"Neither do we," Clint said.

"You first-timers are just trying to make it harder for an old guy like me," Garfield said. "I hope you don't start taking this serious."

"Doc says there's a lot of good money in this, Hammer," Clint said.

"That a fact? Maybe we should think about this some, Clint."

"I'm gonna buy you fellas another beer just to shut you up," Doc said, and got up to go to the bar.

"You see his hands?" Hammer asked.

"Did you see them when he was shooting?" Clint asked. "They're rock steady with the rifle in them."

"How long can that last?" Hammer asked. "How old is he, anyway? I heard stories about him when I was a kid."

"He's got to be over sixty, maybe near seventy," Clint said.

"This may be his last contest."

"And we're here to muck it up," Clint said.

They suspended the conversation when Doc returned with the beers.

"They must have posted the complete list of second-rounders, by now," he said. "We could go on over and check and see who we're up against."

"I understand there's a boxing match set for tonight, too," Clint said.

"Well, let's finish these up and walk over," Hammer said. "Nothing I like better than watching two white men beating up on each other."

"What if one of them is black?" Doc Garfield asked.

"Then we can bet on the outcome, Doc," Hammer said.

"I'll take the black man."

"Why?" Hammer asked.

"White men can't fight a lick in the ring," Doc said, "and you black fellas have hard heads."

"Well," Hammer said, "I'm glad there wasn't any bigotry involved in your decision."

"I ain't no bigot," Doc Garfield said. "I've got the same disregard for *all* people."

Chapter Twenty-Eight

There was a chalkboard erected in the part of the meadow where the first round of shooting had been held, and Doc Garfield was trying to read it, standing as close to it as he could get.

"I can see fine far away but I can't see shit close up," he complained. "What's that say, boy?"

Clint and Hammer didn't know which of them Garfield was referring to—the old man was, after all, *not* a bigot—so Clint stepped up to the board and read off forty-seven names, including Doc's, Hammer's, Whit Black's, Ollie Wish's, Bill Wren's—it was written as "Billy" Wren—and Clint's. Also written in was K.C. Burke.

"Most of them have got to be sodbusters and cowpokes," Doc said. "I recognize a few professionals, like Allie Lange and Jimmy Moss. They're good boys and should be there at the end."

"What about Black and Wish?" Clint asked.

"From what I saw this afternoon, I'd say they'll be there at the end, too, along with that K.C. Burke. Then there'll be you, me, and Hammer, here. A couple of others might get lucky, but their luck will run out. No offense, Hammer, but I'd predict that old

Clint and me are gonna go down to the wire in this one."

"No offense taken," Hammer assured the older man.

"What say we go and watch that boxing match?" Garfield suggested.

At that moment Clint saw Sheriff Wade Barker, flanked by Charlie Taker and a deputy.

"There he is, Sheriff," Taker said, contriving to sound as outraged as he could. "Arrest him!"

There were some other people in the area and they turned to see what was going on.

"He marched into my office bold as brass and robbed me!" Taker said aloud.

"Mister," Wade Barker said to Hammer, "you got to come with me."

"What for?"

"What do you mean, what for?" Barker asked. "We don't stand for strangers comin' into town and robbin' our citizens."

"I didn't rob anyone."

"Mr. Taker says you did."

"He's a liar," Hammer said, looking right into Taker's eyes.

"Search him, Sheriff," Taker said. "He can't have had time to get rid of the money. Search him!"

"Will you stand still for a search?" Barker asked Hammer.

"Only to prove that I'm innocent," Hammer said.

He raised his hands over his head and the sheriff patted him down, checking his pockets.

"Nothing, Mr. Taker."

Not to be outdone Taker said, "Search his friends. He must have given it to them."

"Sheriff," Clint said, "when did this supposed robbery take place?"

"This afternoon, after the shooting competition was over."

"Where?"

"In Mr. Taker's office."

"Well, you see, there's some mistake here," Clint said.

"What do you mean?"

"Mr. Hammer's been with us since then," Clint said, looking at Doc Garfield.

"That's right," Garfield said. "Must be some other big black dude robbed Mr. Taker, here."

"There aren't any other big black men in town," Barker said.

"Search his friends," Taker said. "He must have given the money to one of them to hold."

Barker looked at Clint and said, "I'm afraid you'll have to stand for a search."

Clint looked at the deputy, who was as young as Barker. He was giving Clint a mean-eyed look and his hand was hovering near his gun.

"I'll tell you what, Sheriff," Clint said. "You tell your deputy there to take his hand away from his gun and you can search us."

Barker looked at his deputy and said sharply, "Put your hand down, Leo."

"Aw, Wade . . ." the deputy complained, but he dropped his hand to his side.

Clint raised his hands over his head and said, "Come ahead, Sheriff."

Barker patted Clint down, then did the same to Doc Garfield. Both times he came up empty.

"Nothing, Mr. Taker," he said, apologetically.

"Well, you've got my word that he robbed me," Taker argued. "Isn't that enough?"

"Not with two witnesses who say he was somewhere else," Clint said. "A judge would throw it right out of court, and the sheriff here might lose his job for false arrest."

"He won't lose his—" Taker began, then stopped short of admitting that the sheriff worked for him.

"What do you say, Sheriff?" Clint asked. "Can we go on about our business?"

Confused about what to do, Wade Barker looked at Charles Taker for guidance, and Clint detected an almost imperceptible nod from the man.

"All right," the sheriff said, "go on about your business."

"Thank you," Clint said. "We're going to watch the boxing exhibition; if that's all right with you?"

"I don't care what you do," Barker said.

He said something about getting back to work and left with his deputy in tow, looking back over his shoulder once or twice.

When the lawman and his deputy were gone, Taker confronted Clint and Hammer and Doc and said, "You won't get away with this."

"With what?" Clint asked.

"You're going to find out who owns this town," Taker said to the three of them, and then turned on his heel and left.

"Let's go and see that fight," Doc said, and Hammer and Clint agreed.

"It was a good thing your friend Diehl came in when he did," Hammer said, while they were walking to the tent where the fight was to be held.

As they were getting ready to leave the saloon, Diehl had come in and Clint got the idea of giving him the money to hold. When it was explained to him what was at stake, he was only too glad to help.

"Yep, I guess it was," Clint said.

Chapter Twenty-Nine

As it turned out, there were no black boxers involved in the five matches that were put on, but that didn't stop Doc and Hammer from betting. They were dead even going into the final bout and decided to hike their bet so that one of them would come out well ahead.

"Twenty dollars?" Doc said.

"You're on!" Hammer said.

"I think I've had enough of this," Clint said. "If you fellas don't mind I'll be going back to the hotel."

"You take the bed," Doc said, "I been sleeping on the floor anyway."

"You two are sharing a room?" Hammer asked.

"Sort of," Doc said. "It's a long and sad story, my friend . . ."

"I've got all night," Clint heard Hammer say as he left the tent.

Walking back to the hotel, Clint found himself wishing he had run into Carol Sydney tonight. He thought it was time they cleared up their differences. He especially wanted to tell her that he had no intentions of holding her to the deal they'd made.

Clint heard the shot and felt the pain in his shoulder at about the same time. He threw himself to the ground and rolled. From wherever the shot had been fired it probably looked as if he'd been seriously hit, because somebody let out a whoop of pleasure.

Clint kept rolling and came to a stop underneath the nearest boardwalk, in the dark, and lay still. He had no idea how badly he was hit, but now was not the time to find out.

Now was the time to survive.

"What was that?" Doc Garfield asked.

"What was what?" Hammer said.

"I heard a shot."

"I didn't hear anything."

"Well, my eyes may be going, son, but my ears ain't," Doc Garfield said. He headed for the tent exit and said, "That was a damned shot!"

"You're just leaving because my fighter's winning," Hammer accused him, but he followed the older man anyway.

Clint lay still beneath the boardwalk, slipping his gun from his holster. He was hoping that the shooter would come down to survey his work, but after a few moments it became obvious that he wasn't. Apparently, whoever had fired was convinced he'd made a killing shot, and there was no need to follow it up.

That meant he was an amateur, because that mistake was going to cost him, dearly.

". . . tell you I heard a shot," Clint heard Doc Garfield saying.

"And I say you're trying to weasel out of our bet," Hammer said.

"Would you two stop arguing and get me out of here!" Clint shouted.

"What the hell was that?" Hammer demanded.

"Under here!" Clint said.

"Clint?"

The two men bent over and then grabbed hold of him and pulled him out.

"You hit, boy?" Garfield asked.

"I'm pretty sure I was, yeah," Clint said.

"Sit still, then, and let me take a look."

Clint sat right in the street while Doc inspected him for wounds.

"Check the shoulder," Clint said, "the left one."

"Turn toward the light—I see it."

Clint jumped as Doc poked at the wound.

"It's clean," the old man said. "In fact, it was almost a clean miss. Dug a furrow out of your shoulder, is all. Come on, Hammer," Doc said, grabbing Clint's right arm. "Let's haul this fella to his feet and get him to a doctor for some patchin' up."

They lifted Clint to his feet and started walking with him between them. Clint holstered his gun. The shock had worn off, and the shoulder was starting to hurt.

"Did you see who shot you?" Doc asked.

"No, it was from behind," Clint said, and as he said it he suddenly became angrier than he'd been in some time. "From behind, damn it! Can you believe it?"

"Take it easy, Clint," Hammer said. "That's the way some of us are gonna get it, that's all. We've got to live with that."

"Living with it isn't a problem," Clint said. "*Dying* with it is what I'm worried about."

"You didn't see or hear anything?" Doc Garfield asked.

"I heard a whoop of joy when he thought he hit me solid," Clint said.

"That ain't much help," Hammer said.

"Maybe not," Clint said, "but if I hear that particular whoop again, I'll remember it."

"Ain't much to go on," Doc said.

"It's all I'll need," Clint said. "That son of a bitch is going to be a sorry son of a bitch when I catch up to him. You can bet on that!"

"Calm down," Hammer said.

"Calm down, shit!" Clint said, but got hold of himself and did start to calm down.

"How did you fellas know something was wrong?"

"The old codger here," Hammer said, "has got ears like a cat. He heard the shot."

"Glad your ears are still working, Doc."

"I don't care if they're working or not," Hammer said, "all I know is he owes me twenty dollars. My fighter was about to put his man away when he went running out of the tent."

"The bet was off as soon as the shot was fired," Garfield said.

"Bullshit," Hammer said, "a bet's a bet."

"Well then, you go back and find out who won."

"What do you mean, who won? My man won."

"We don't know that for sure," Garfield said, "and I ain't payin' off without knowin'."

"Maybe you two better let me go to the doctor myself," Clint said. "In my weakened condition this arguing is going to kill me before loss of blood does!"

•   •   •

"It's not bad," he said. "It shouldn't even restrict your movements too much."

"Thanks, Doc," Clint said, putting on his shirt.

"Are you sure you can't tell me anything about the man who shot you?" Sheriff Wade Barker asked.

Clint looked at Hammer and Doc before he answered Barker.

"Sheriff," he said, "I can't even tell you for sure that it was a man."

"Then there's nothing I can do for you."

"I'll bet that just breaks your heart," Clint said buttoning his shirt.

"No, Adams," Barker said, "what breaks my heart is that he missed!"

"Well, if it's a body you're looking for," Clint said, "when I find him—and I will—you'll have one."

"I don't stand for murder in my town, Adams."

"Except when it suits you, huh?" Clint said. "What about Charles Taker? Why don't you check and see where he was when I was shot?"

"Mr. Taker is a respected member of this town—"

"Boy," Doc Garfield said, "Charles Taker *is* this town, and you're insulting our intelligence by pretending otherwise."

"You three just better stay out of trouble," Barker said, pointing to each of them in turn, "or you'll be looking at the inside of my jail."

Barker turned and stormed out of the office.

"Tough little dude," Hammer said. "Doesn't *he* think so?"

"What do I owe you, Doc?" Clint asked. The doctor told him and he paid his bill.

Outside the office Clint said, "Well, I'm going back to the hotel this time for sure."

"Why don't you go over to Diane's?" Garfield suggested. "If they tried for you in the street, they might try again in your room."

"Good thought, Doc, but then you better sleep somewhere else."

"Hell, no," Garfield said, "I was thinking of giving that hotel bed a try tonight." He looked at Hammer and said, "You happy with the livery, or you want to try the floor in my room?"

"Sounds good," Hammer said.

"You fellas don't have to put your lives on the line for me," Clint said.

"Don't make it sound like more than it is, Adams," Hammer said. "This man's offering me a chance to get out of that stinking livery, and I'm taking it."

"Suit yourself."

"By the way," Hammer said.

"What?" Clint said.

"Who's Diane?"

Clint turned to walk away and heard Doc say, "It's a long story..."

Chapter Thirty

When Clint showed up at Diane's door, she opened it sleepily and admitted him. When she saw that he was hurt she gave him just the right amount of sympathy, but didn't fawn over him, which he appreciated.

She also stripped him, set him down on the bed, and then slithered down between his legs to take his mind off the pain in his shoulder.

He appreciated that, too.

Charles Taker was livid.

"All right," he said to Barker, "get out!"

"Mr. Taker—"

"Get out, Barker. You haven't been much use to me today!"

"There was nothing I could do, Mr. Taker—"

"I know," Taker said, "I know." He decided to back off a bit. "It's all right, Wade, I'm just a little tired is all."

"What do I do about this attempt on Adam's life, Mr. Taker?"

"He can't give you any information on the shooter, Wade. Just forget it. There's nothing you can do."

"Yes, sir."

"Go and get some sleep."

"Yes, sir. Thank you."

After Barker left, Taker swiveled around in his chair to look down at the darkened town, lit only by the yellowish glow of the occasional street lamp.

Which of those idiots had decided to take matters into their own hands early? It showed the brains those nitwits had that one of them thought that shooting the Gunsmith in the back would enhance his own reputation.

What really angered Taker was that the buffoon had missed!

Doc Garfield and Fred Hammer set watches, with Hammer taking the first. He'd wake Garfield in four hours. If the man who had shot Clint tried again tonight, he was in for a huge surprise.

Hammer looked with amusement as the old man tried to get comfortable in the bed when he was so used to sleeping on the ground.

"Shit," Doc Garfield finally said, throwing back the bedclothes, "the bed is yours Hammer. I'm too old to start sleeping comfortable now."

Hammer sat on the edge of the bed with his gunbelt hanging on the bedpost and waited for his watch to end.

Carol Sydney scolded herself for the hundredth time that day.

She could have made the first move toward Clint and cleared up the differences between them, but she hadn't. Instead she'd acted stuck-up and made the situation worse.

Actually, if Clint succeeded in winning the contest, she was perfectly willing to pay off on her promise.

That she wondered, though, was if he would accept payment.

Diane sat atop Clint, riding him, being careful not to jostle his shoulder, but as she approached orgasm she bounced on him mindlessly, causing him to bite his lip in pain—and then he erupted inside of her, and the pain was once again lost in the pleasure.

Later she asked, "Do you think they'll try again?"

"They tried once, they can always try again."

"Who do you think it was?"

"Somebody working for Taker—but I don't think Taker knew about this."

"Why do you say that?"

"For everything he is, I don't think he's the kind of man who'd condone back-shooting. Oh, if I *was* dead as a result of it, he wouldn't shed a tear, but I don't think it's the way he'd want it done, if he had a choice."

"How would he want it done?"

"Face-to-face, fair, so that there'd be no questions."

"Can that be done?" she asked. "I mean, you *are* the fastest—I mean, your reputation—"

"It doesn't matter what your reputation is, Diane," he said, interrupting her, "there's always somebody out there with the capability to kill you, fair and square."

"Maybe you'll never meet that someone."

"That's always a possibility, too," he said, and then added, "and a much preferable one."

Whit Black looked down at the top of the blonde head of the whore who was sucking him. She was doing a fairly good job, but he still couldn't help wondering who had taken the back shot at the Gunsmith earlier that evening.

He'd heard about it from an irate Charlie Taker, who told Black that he was going to have to keep the others in line. The try for Adams' reputation was supposed to take place *after* the shoot.

Black reached for the whore's head to slow her down. She was going too fast, now.

"Easy, baby," he said, and she muttered something and began sliding her mouth over him in long, slow movements.

"That's it," he said, moving his hips in unison with her bobbing head.

Black knew that *he* hadn't taken the shot, and he felt sure that Ollie Wish hadn't. For one thing, if it had been one of them, they wouldn't have missed— but neither of them would ever back-shoot a man.

Now McQuirk, he might, given the right circumstances, but Black's money was on Kenny Last. The kid was upset that he had been forced out of the competition so soon. Maybe he was mad enough to do something stupid.

Black would have to talk to him tomorrow.

"Oh, yes, sweet girl," he said to the girl, "that's it, you're getting it now . . . yessss!"

• • •

The man who *had* taken the shot at Clint Adams still thought that Adams was dead. He wouldn't find out that he'd made a terrible error—in judgment and execution—until the next morning.

For now he felt immensely satisfied with himself, and was already counting the money Charles Taker was going to pay him—not to mention the money that Whit Black's plan was going to make for all of them.

To hell with the fucking contest!

Chapter Thirty-One

The second round of shooting went just about the way Doc Garfield figured. The shooters who had lucked through the first round fell by the wayside fairly quickly.

The second round consisted of shooting at round glass balls that were thrown into the air. The techniques varied from tracking it and shooting it as it flew upward, to marking it at its apex and then shooting it on the way down.

Clint pretty much depended on his reflexes. Many of the men who failed did so because they were trying to aim at the damned things. Clint just drew his gun and pointed as if he were pointing his finger, and fired.

They were to shoot at twenty-five balls, and he hit every one.

Other perfect rounds were shot by Hammer, Doc Garfield, Whit Black, Ollie Wish, K.C. Burke, Jimmy Moss, Allie Lange and—a surprise to all— Billy Wren.

The field had been narrowed down very quickly.

"Folks," the head judge called out, "we'll start our third round in about an hour, to give the contestants time to rest. All shooters, be back on your marks in one hour, or you'll be eliminated."

"It's going pretty much the way you predicted, Doc," Hammer said. "I'm impressed. Where do you say I'm going to finish?"

"Third," Garfield said without hesitation, "behind Clint and me."

"In that order?"

"Of course," Doc Garfield said. "I didn't come all this way to lose this thing."

Clint laughed and turned and bumped right into Billy Wren.

"Nice shoot, Wren," he said.

Wren looked surprised at the words, then said, "Thanks, Adams."

"Complimenting the competition, Clint?" Hammer asked.

"He's playing mind games with the boy."

"Just telling the truth," Clint said. "You fellas ought to try it some time."

"Can't teach an old dog, Clint," Doc Garfield said. "How's your shoulder, by the way."

"It's sore, but I'll live. Anything interesting happen in my room last night?"

"Nothing," Hammer said. "We split watches, and we both could have slept."

"How about you?" Garfield asked. "Anything unusual happen in Diane's room last night?"

"You're a dirty old man, Doc," Clint said.

"Ain't it the sad truth. Anybody for a beer?"

"You want to get us drunk so we can't see straight?" Hammer asked.

"I want to get a beer to wet my throat. You don't want me to buy you one, just say so."

"Oh, he's buying," Hammer said to Clint.

"We better go with him, then," Clint said. "No telling when this spell will come over him again."

"You fellas is born jokers," Garfield said. "I'm laughin' so hard my sides are splittin'. Come on, young 'uns, I'll show you how a man drinks."

Clint, Hammer, and Garfield were sitting in the saloon when Diane suddenly came running in, obviously upset about something.

"What is it, Diane?" Clint asked.

"It's my father, Clint," Diane said, crying. "He's been hurt, hurt badly."

"Where is he?"

"The doctor's."

"Let's go," he said, rising and grabbing her by the arm.

"Wait a minute," Hammer shouted. "Who's her father?"

"Tom Diehl!" Clint replied over his shoulder.

Hammer looked at Garfield, who was standing up, saying, "Well, let's go!"

"He's taken a bad beating," the doctor said.

"How bad?" Clint asked.

"He probably has some broken ribs, maybe a concussion. I know he's got a broken arm, and he might have a busted collarbone. I'll have to keep him here for a while to be sure of the extent of his injuries. He may be bleeding inside."

Diane was standing within the circle of Clint's arm, and she pressed against him more and more with each of the doctor's words.

"Can we talk to him?" Clint asked.

"No, I'm sorry, he's in no condition to talk."

"Just a couple of questions."

"He couldn't answer them," the doctor said. "He's very disoriented."

Clint felt Hammer's hand come down on his shoulder.

"We better let the man do his job, Clint."

"Hammer's right, Diane," Clint said, holding her tighter. "Let's go somewhere and talk."

Outside Diane suddenly pushed away from him.

"I don't want to go somewhere and talk!" she snapped. "We all know who's responsible for this."

"Who?" Hammer asked.

"Taker, that's who. He must have found out about the businesses my father owns, and he wants to get him out of the way."

"We don't know that Taker's responsible for this, Diane—"

"Maybe *you* don't know," she said, "but I do, and if you won't do something about it, I will!"

She stormed away from them and Doc Garfield put his hand on Clint's arm to keep him from going after her.

"Give her some time to cool off, son."

"Could she be right?" Hammer asked. "Could it be Taker who had Diehl beaten up."

"It could be," Clint said, and relayed to Hammer Tom Diehl's past with Charles Taker.

"Maybe we should go and ask him," Hammer said.

"Maybe one of us should," Clint said.

"That one of us being you?" Hammer asked.

Clint nodded.

"I'll walk along with you and wait outside," Hammer said.

"I got nothin' better to do before the shoot starts again," Doc said. He looked at Clint and said, "We will make it back to our marks for the third round?"

"We'll be there," Clint assured him.

"Well, then, let's go and see the man!"

Chapter Thirty-Two

Taker was looking out his window when he saw Clint Adams, Fred Hammer, and Doc Garfield coming down the street toward his office. He watched, looking straight down at them, while Hammer and Garfield stayed outside, and Clint Adams went inside, presumably to come up to his office.

Taker turned around, sat down behind his desk, opened his top drawer, touched the gun that was sitting there, and then closed the door and waited for the knock on the door.

It never came.

Clint considered knocking on the door first, but then decided to simply shove it open.

"People usually knock," Charles Taker said to him, as Clint stood in the open doorway.

"Tell me about you and Tom Diehl."

Taker frowned.

"Tom Diehl? What about him?"

"He's over at the doctor's, beaten up very badly." Clint said.

"How badly?"

"Didn't your men report to you on that?"

"My men?" Taker said. "What are you talking about?"

"Let's put it all out on the table so we can see it, Taker," Clint said. "Did you have Diehl beaten up?"

"Why would I have Tom Diehl beaten up?"

"Isn't he your ex-partner?"

"Well, sure—"

"Didn't you swindle him out of his share of what is now your fortune?"

"Whoa, wait a minute," Taker said. "Everything I have I earned—"

"And some of it you took from Diehl."

"If Tom Diehl wasn't strong enough to keep what he had—"

"So now that you see him once again amassing some holdings—"

"Holdings? What holdings?"

"You're going to tell me that you didn't know that he owned several businesses in town?"

"Diehl? He owns the livery stable. What the hell are you talking about, Adams? What businesses does he own?"

Clint stared at Taker, who seemed genuinely surprised by what he was saying. Was it possible that he knew nothing of what happened? And if that was true, had Clint just revealed everything Tom Diehl and his daughter had been trying to keep secret?

"You didn't have Diehl beaten up?"

"Believe me, Adams," Taker said, "if I did, I'd take credit for it." The man frowned now and asked, "How badly is Tom hurt?"

"We don't know yet. The doc says he may have some broken ribs, some internal bleeding, maybe a concussion. He's got a couple of broken bones—"

Taker surprised Clint by standing up quickly and coming around the desk.

"Where are you going?" he asked.

"To see him," Taker said. "He's going to have some heavy doctor bills. I want to tell the doctor that I'll take care of them."

Now it was Clint's turn to frown.

"Why would you do that?"

"We were partners once, Adams."

"But you cheated him—"

"If I did—and I'm not saying I did—that was business. That doesn't mean I want him dead."

"I'll walk over there with you—"

"Don't you have a contest to shoot in?" Taker asked.

Clint remembered the shoot, which was probably just moments away from starting. He didn't want to miss it, and he didn't want to be the cause of Hammer and Garfield missing it, but he couldn't just let Taker go over to the doctor's office without warning him.

"If you try anything, Taker—"

"All I'm going to do is what I said," Taker said.

As Taker went past him, Clint grabbed his arm and looked into his eyes.

"What about the attempt on me last night?"

"I had nothing to do with that," Taker said, shaking off Clint's hold.

The answer came too quick, as if it was true and Taker got some satisfaction out of being able to say so. He was inclined to believe Taker. He was also inclined to believe that the man who'd tried to kill him was one of Taker's men who had gone ahead without his boss's okay.

"Now if you'll leave my office I'd like to lock up before *I* leave."

Clint left and walked downstairs ahead of Taker while he locked his door. He was standing downstairs with Hammer and Garfield when Taker came down. The man did not give them a second look as he strode past and headed for the doctor's office.

"Where's he going?" Hammer asked.

"I'll tell you on the way," Clint said. "We don't want to miss our mark."

As they hurried down the street toward the meadow, Clint wondered if he should have warned Taker to watch out for Diane. He still didn't know that she was Tom Diehl's daughter.

Chapter Thirty-Three

Clint was preoccupied throughout the next round of shooting, but he hit all of his targets nevertheless.

This round was a duplicate of the first round, only they were shooting at fifty balls this time rather than twenty-five.

When the round was finished there were five men left: Clint Adams, Doc Garfield, Fred Hammer, K.C. Burke, and Whit Black.

"I'm surprised," Garfield said.

"At what?" Clint asked.

"I'm the only regular left."

"Well," Fred Hammer said, "maybe those regulars only made it to the final round contest after contest because Clint and I have never competed before."

Garfield pointed a finger at Hammer and said, "You think you're joking, but that's probably the case."

"Maybe they just had an off day," Clint said.

"Or maybe they was intimidated."

"By what?" Clint asked.

"By a couple of big reps."

Both Hammer and Clint made a show of looking around them, and then said to Garfield—in unison —"Who?"

169

"Very funny, but think about it. These boys have never shot against anybody more fearful than . . . than me, and now you two are here."

"Maybe we're just better shots, Doc," Hammer said.

Frowning, Doc said, "Well, sure, there is that possibility."

"When's the next round?" Hammer asked.

"They'll set it up right away," Garfield said. "A hundred balls. Whoever hits the most wins."

"You've done this many times before Doc," Hammer said. "How many hits does it take to win?"

"On the average I'd say you'd have a good chance with ninety-eight out of a hundred."

"Ninety-eight," Hammer repeated, nodding.

"Ordinarily."

"What do you man, ordinarily."

"Those are contests without the Gunsmith entered," Garfield said. "Today, I'd say you're gonna have to be damn near perfect."

Clint heard every word they were saying, but he wasn't really listening. He was thinking about Tom Diehl, Charles Taker . . . *and* he was wondering where Diane was.

Off to one side Whit Black and Ollie Wish stood, talking and watching Clint, Hammer, and Garfield.

"Adams ain't gonna be easy to take with those other two around," Ollie Wish said.

"Hammer's the one to worry about," Black said. "The old man's just a contest shooter."

"What do we do, then?"

"Let's do a little pushing and see how far they'll take it."

"Adams?"

"Naw, just the old man and the black guy."

"How far do we take it?" Wish asked.

"As far as it will go, Ollie," Black said, "just remember to let the big guy pull first—and tell McQuirk and Last that! They wait for him to move!"

"Anybody know who this K.C. Burke is?" Fred Hammer asked.

Garfield shook his head.

"He's a young fella. I've never seen him in a contest before."

"Clint?" Hammer said. "Hey, Clint?"

"I heard you. What?"

"K.C. Burke. Ever hear of him?"

"Not a whisper."

Hammer looked at Garfield again and said, "And how good is Whit Black?"

"Don't know," Garfield said. "It's his first contest, too."

"So four of us are new, and you're the old veteran," Hammer said.

"I guess so," Garfield said. "I guess I'll have to teach you newcomers how it's done."

"Hey, Pop!" a man's voice called out.

Clint saw Garfield's eyes turn cold as flint just before he turned his head to look at Whit Black.

"You talkin' to me, sonny?" Doc asked.

"Yeah, I'm talking to you," Black said. He was standing there with Ollie Wish by his side—Wish, who had missed once during round three—and off to one side he was backed up by two other men, Jamie McQuirk and Kenny Last.

Those four were pretty tight, and Clint had become fairly sure they were working for Taker, especially since he'd seen both Black and Wish come out of his office.

"Why don't you step aside and let the young men show you how to shoot, Pops?" Whit Black asked. "You're getting in the way."

"And I'm gonna get even more in your way, friend," Doc Garfield said. "Right between you and that prize money."

"You're just making it take longer, Pop," Black said. "Why don't you take your body guard and let me and the Gunsmith shoot it out."

Now it was Hammer whose eyes turned cold.

Clint could see what they were trying to do. They were trying to get Garfield and Hammer to make a move on them. Apparently, Black and his cohorts felt sure they could take the two men.

That would leave him—the Gunsmith—standing alone against them.

That is, if things went as they planned.

Clint abruptly moved in front of Garfield and Hammer, both of whom were glaring at Whit Black.

"This ain't your fight, Adams," Black said quickly.

"So far," Clint said, "I don't see a fight. I just see four yellow polecats trying to force a play from two men so they can gun them down."

"Why would we want to do that?" Whit Black asked.

"Well, I'll tell you," Clint said, "I do have a theory on that, Black. You want to hear it?"

"Sure, go ahead. We got a few minutes."

"I think the four of you are cowards."

"What?" Black said, stiffening. Clint could also see Kenny Last and Jamie McQuirk straighten up.

The only one who didn't take offense was Ollie Wish. He was older, and knew better.

"Whit—" he said, but Black shook him off.

"You better explain yourself, Adams," he said to Clint.

"You and your friends came here to try me out, Black," Clint said. "If one of you kills me—and this is a theory, mind you—I think you all get paid off."

"By who?"

"Charlie Taker, who else? I understand Charlie's got a pretty checkered past. He must have met up with you four at some time or other, and he called you all here because I was getting in his way."

"That's an interesting theory."

"I'm not done," Clint said. "You fellas expected a four against one, but you didn't count on me having some friends here. Now you're trying to get Hammer and Doc here *out* of the way so it can be four against one again. I'd call that cowardly, wouldn't you?"

Whit Black's eyes took on a murderous glaze.

"Whit, don't," Ollie said. "He's trying to push you—"

"Come on, Black," Clint said. "Three against four, that still gives you the edge, doesn't it? Let's see you make your play right here and now."

"Make it four against four," a voice said. Clint turned his head slightly and saw K.C. Burke move in next to Garfield. "I never did like uneven odds," the younger man said.

"There you have it, Black," Clint said. "You've got the deal."

A crowd had gathered to listen to the talk, and now that there was gunplay in the offing they scattered for cover. Clint didn't see them, as he was concentrating on Black, but they sounded like a herd of cattle stampeding.

"Whit, I'm tellin' ya," Ollie Wish said, "this ain't the time."

"Come on, young folk," Garfield said, calling out to McQuirk and Last, "come join the party."

"It's dyin' time!" Hammer chimed in.

Hammer and Garfield flanked Clint and waited.

Jamie McQuirk was the first one to give it up and walk away. When Kenny Last saw him walk away, he followed.

"Whit—" Wish said, grabbing Black's arm. "Let's go!"

"What about the contest, Whit?" Clint called out as Black allowed himself to be led away by the older and wiser Ollie Wish.

"Fuck the contest, and you!" Whit Black called out.

"Well, gentlemen," Clint said to the others, "it looks like it's just the four of us."

"Jesus," Hammer said, "you don't cut a man any slack, do you?"

"One of them back-shot me, or tried to," Clint said.

"Which one?" K.C. Burke asked.

"I figure the first one to give it up was yellow enough to have tried it."

"That makes it McQuirk," Hammer said.

"I guess."

"You gonna let him go?"

"I don't think they're leaving town just yet," Clint said. "Besides, the four of *us* have some unfinished business, don't we?"

Chapter Thirty-Four

Suddenly it was Ollie Wish who was in charge.

"You're a coward," Whit Black said to Jamie McQuirk.

"You're a fool," McQuirk said to Black. "We all are if we think we can outdraw the Gunsmith. Have you seen him shoot during this contest? The man doesn't even aim. Jesus, for us to think—"

"You're yella!" Black shouted.

"You're not the Gunsmith, Black," McQuirk said. "I wouldn't mind trying you—"

"Shut up, both of you!" Ollie Wish shouted.

Shocked, both Black and McQuirk fell silent.

"If you two can keep from killing each other for a minute, you'd see that this is our chance. Everyone is in the meadow watching the final round of the contest."

"So?" Kenny Last said.

"So, the bank is ours for the taking. Can't be more than a teller and a manager inside, and the law's got to be watching the contest, too. Can't be more than deputy in town." Ollie Wish looked at Black and said, "Forget everything else, Whit, and you'll see that I'm right."

"All right," Black said after a moment, "you are right, Ollie. Let's take the bank."

"Kenny," Wish said to the youngest of the four, "go and get the horses. We won't come out until we see you out front with the horses."

"Ollie—" Last began to complain.

"Somebody's got to get the horses, Kenny!" Ollie said. "If we all do our part, we'll leave town rich men!"

"All right, Ollie," Kenny said.

As the young man headed for the livery Ollie said, "Let's get over to that bank."

Charles Taker was returning from the doctor's office, where he had promised to handle all of Tom Diehl's bills. He had no idea who had beaten Diehl up that way, but he was sorry it had happened. For all the trouble that had passed between him and Diehl, Taker was surprised to find that he still liked his ex-partner.

If he knew who had beaten him he'd—

He stopped short when he saw Kenny Last riding down the street leading three saddled horses.

Obviously, Black, Wish, and the others were leaving town, but why was Kenny leading all the horses? And where were the others?

Taker stepped into a doorway so Kenny Last wouldn't see him, and watched to see where the young man was going. It took only a few moments for him to figure it out.

The bank!

While everyone was watching the final round of the Takersville Shoot, Whit Black, Ollie Wish, Jamie

McQuirk, and Kenny Last were holding up the Takersville Bank!

As quickly as he could, Taker skimmed the storefronts, hurrying to his office. He ran up the stairs, unlocked the door, and hurried to his desk, where he took his gun from the top drawer. From his window he could see the bank, and Kenny Last was now in front of it with all of the horses.

Taker hurried down the stairs. If those fools thought he was going to let them rob the bank—his bank!—they had a surprise coming to them.

Chapter Thirty-Five

Coincidence had a lot to do with it.

As luck would have it, all four competitors were reloading at the same time when they heard the barrage of shots coming from town.

Clint looked around and saw Sheriff Barker standing on the sidelines, watching the contest. The man seemed frozen in his tracks.

"Come on," Barker shouted to the others, and started running toward town. He was thinking about Diane. He had no inkling as to what they'd find when they reached town.

Taker's first shot took Kenny Last in the shoulder. As soon as he fired he knew he'd made a mistake. As the others were coming out of the bank he should have shot either Whit Black or Ollie Wish. It had been a long time since Charlie Taker had had a gun in his hand in a situation like this.

Whit Black and Ollie Wish reacted immediately, with McQuirk just a second behind them. They began firing at Taker, and as their bullets struck him he seemed to dance in the street. Finally, they stopped firing and he dropped to the ground.

"Reload!" Ollie Wish shouted.

"What for? He's dead!" McQuirk said.

"Do you hear that?" Wish asked.

"I don't hear nothing!" McQuirk said.

"That's right," Wish said. "We don't hear any shooting from the meadow, which means they must have heard ours. Reload!"

Clint and Hammer reached the scene first. Doc Garfield couldn't keep up with them, and not too many others had taken up after them. If there was shooting going on in town, most of the people in the meadow wanted to stay there.

Taker was already down, and they really didn't even see him. They saw Black, Wish, McQuirk, and what looked like an injured Kenny Last sitting astride their horses outside the bank. Black and Wish had bags in their hands, obviously filled with money.

"Hold it!" Clint shouted.

"Hold it?" Hammer echoed. "Jesus, announce—" he started to say when the four bank robbers started firing at them.

"You think you're still a damned lawman?" Hammer demanded, and they both broke for cover.

They drew and started firing. Clint's first shot struck Jamie McQuirk and yanked him from his saddle. Hammer fired, and Kenny Last's body jerked with the impact of the bullets, and then fell from his horse.

"Let's go! Let's go!" Ollie Wish shouted, but Whit Black had his own ideas.

As Wish rode down the street away from them, Whit Black continued firing at Clint and Hammer.

Both of them stood up and fired at him together. Their shots caught him square in the chest and as blood gushed from his mouth, he dropped his gun and the money sack and slid from his horse to the ground.

"Wish is getting away!" Hammer said. He took a few steps forward—as if that would bring him within range—and pointed his gun.

"Don't waste the bullet," Clint said. "He's out of range. We'll have to get a couple of horses."

"Don't bother, boys," Doc Garfield said, having finally caught up to them. "Leave him to me."

Doc, winded but hands steady, raised the Sharps to his shoulder and sighted along the barrel. Ollie Wish was rapidly becoming a smaller and smaller target. Doc took his time, made sure the shot was lined up right, and fired.

For a moment they thought he had missed, but then suddenly Ollie Wish looked as if he had leaped from his saddle.

"Bull's-eye," Doc Garfield said, grinning.

Chapter Thirty-Six

Charles William Taker died a hero.

The townspeople never suspected that it was he who had brought the four would-be bank robbers to town in the first place. They seemed to have forgotten what they heard in the meadow, when Clint had been goading Whit Black.

As far as the contest was concerned, both Clint and Hammer withdrew from it, leaving Doc to shoot against young K.C. Burke.

After a hundred balls they were even, having missed one a piece. They had to shoot fifty-eight more balls before K.C. Burke finally missed another one, and Doc Garfield was declared the winner of the Takersville Shoot.

In the absence of the late Charles Taker, the bank paid Doc the prize money.

Tom Diehl regained consciousness and told the doctor that he'd been attacked by two strangers, who had then robbed him.

"They didn't get much, and I guess that got them mad, so they took it out on me. Lucky I was unconscious at the time." Diehl was going to be fine.

Immediately following the contest, Carol Sydney approached Clint.

"I'm glad you withdrew," she said.

"Well, I figured with Taker dead you wouldn't have any trouble getting an extension from the bank."

"I won't have any trouble, you're right."

"How did your boys do?"

"We won half the events," she said, "and they made some money. To a man they want to split it fifty-fifty with me."

"They're good boys."

"They are. Um, I guess we don't have to worry about my paying off my debt."

"I guess not."

"Will you be leaving town now?"

"Probably tomorrow morning."

"Could I persuade you to come out to dinner?" she asked. "I think I have an apology to extend to you, and I have an idea how I'd like to do that."

Diane was going to be pretty busy looking after her father, so Clint said to Carol, "I think I could be persuaded, yeah."

"See you tonight, then."

"Tonight," Clint said.

As Carol rode off, Hammer and Doc approached Clint.

"We've got some drinkin' to do," Garfield said, "and you two have some explainin' to do."

"What kind of explaining?" Hammer asked.

"I want to know why you withdrew from the contest."

"Why, Doc," Clint said, "we knew you'd beat us."

"That's bull!"

"You wouldn't have beaten us?" Hammer asked.

"Hell, yes, but that ain't why you boys quit."

"Doc," Clint said, "target-shooting just isn't our game."

"Drinking, however," Fred Hammer said, "is. Are you buying?"

"Hell," Clint said, "he just won the Great Takersville Shoot, of course he's buying!"